Quintessential Us

The Quad was ablaze with buzz about the Environmental Challenge sponsored by the Fashion Café. Reps from the winning school would naturally attend opening night of the Beverly Hills location. The winning project would like, be put on display there.

I'd been pumped ever since hearing the announcement in class. Ditto for De, who was all "Did you hear, Cher? We'll have a place on the Fashion Café's Wall of Fame and . . ."

I finished De's thought, as I often do. ". . . we'll be rubbing buffed elbows with supermodel-slash-moguls, parading down the catwalk that leads to our exhibit. Tourists will flock to see it! Is this so not the quintessential us?"

De and I were furiously high-fiving each other when Amber broke in with a pronouncement. It rubbed us the way a Calvin in the irregular bin might. It was something like "And I, Amber Salk, will lead us to victory on this project."

Like, what? Amber lead us? How oxymoronic can you get? Or even just plain moronic.

"Excuse me, Major General Salk," I interrupted. "Either I missed the ballot-stuffing or something, but exactly when did *you* get elected queen of the Fashion Café project?"

Clueless™ Books

CLUELESS™
A novel by H. B. Gilmour
Based on the film written and directed by
Amy Heckerling

CLUELESS™: CHER'S GUIDE TO . . . WHATEVER
By H. B. Gilmour

CLUELESS™: ACHIEVING PERSONAL PERFECTION
By H. B. Gilmour

CLUELESS™: AN AMERICAN BETTY IN PARIS
By Randi Reisfeld

CLUELESS™: CHER NEGOTIATES NEW YORK
By Jennifer Baker

CLUELESS™: CHER'S FURIOUSLY FIT WORKOUT
By Randi Reisfeld

CLUELESS™: FRIEND OR FAUX
By H. B. Gilmour

CLUELESS™: CHER GOES ENVIRO-MENTAL
By Randi Reisfeld

Available from ARCHWAY Paperbacks

CLUELESS™

Cher Goes Enviro-Mental

Randi Reisfeld

AN ARCHWAY PAPERBACK
Published by POCKET BOOKS
New York London Toronto Sydney Tokyo Singapore

This book is a work of fiction. Names, characters, places and incidents are products of the author's imagination or are used fictitiously. Any resemblance to actual events or locales or persons, living or dead, is entirely coincidental.

AN ARCHWAY PAPERBACK *Original*

An Archway Paperback published by
POCKET BOOKS, a division of Simon & Schuster Inc.
1230 Avenue of the Americas, New York, NY 10020

™ and Copyright © 1997 by Paramount Pictures

ISBN: 0-671-00324-0

First Archway Paperback printing January 1997

10 9 8 7 6 5 4 3 2 1

AN ARCHWAY PAPERBACK and colophon are registered trademarks of Simon & Schuster Inc.

Printed in the U.S.A.

IL: 7+

Acknowledgments

Snaps to Anne and Fran, for comin' up with the plan.

Props to Susan G. for the eco-jingo and to Rich A. for the law lingo.

Worshipful thanks to Mike M. for untangling computer crisis #99—once again.

Whoo! Whoo! Whoo! to my brutally supportive homies—you-know-who!

Marvin, Stefanie, and Scott: Could I do this without you? Not.

Cher Goes Enviro-Mental

Chapter 1

"It's on the *left,* the side it's always on," I insisted, pointing to the exact spot on my chin where I was furiously certain Shalom Harlow's mole was permanently situated.

"Hello? Only if you were watching through a mirror, Cher. Excuse me, but on last night's *House of Style,* said mole was significantly on the *right.*" Amber Salk, the t.b.—true blue, as in friend—in my life who lived to contradict me, was way passionate on this point. "Which means," she added triumphantly, "it's faux."

"Well, I think I know my supermodels," I said demurely, "but on the subject of faux, I totally bow to your expertise. Amber knows faux . . ."

". . . like Dennis Rodman knows tattoos. Like how faux can you go, Ambulow?" My best friend, De, who was sitting behind me, finished my thought.

"Ouch!"

I thought Amber was reacting to De's subtle diss, but

her hand flew up to her cheek, and she screamed and whirled around. "What the— Who did that?" Amber had taken a hit on her carefully contoured cheekbone with . . . a flying rubber band? Judging by the rampant hysteria coming from the back of our classroom, the flinger, Murray—and the flinger's apprentice, Sean— were both inanely proud of their dubious achievement. They were all pumping fists in the air and "Whoo! Whoo! Whoo-ing," in that ancient Arsenio style.

As everyone in our crowd knows, Murray is De's significant other. And though his Baldwinesque credits *are* majorly praiseworthy, his deficits are piling up. One of which is his profound immaturity, especially when he's hanging with the boy equivalent of a t.b., Sean. Translation: most of the time.

As Amber flew up from her seat and stomped over to Murray, a tiny but determined voice from the front of our classroom room called out good-naturedly, "Take your seats, students, please. Settle down, we have an important new chapter to start today."

The voice belonged to the diminutive but dedicated Miss Geist, our social studies teacher, who, dressed today in a frumpy Talbots shift, was trying to get our attention.

Miss Geist's request was met with its usual level of success: not much. But hello? That's only natural. Aside from Amber and Murray's current contretemps, most students, with the predictable exception of valedictorian-in-waiting Janet Hong, were massively preoccupied. Nails were being buffed, teeth flossed, snacks consumed, naps taken, hair restyled, makeup applied. Just the normal activities you'd expect to find in any sophomore social studies class across the nation.

Miss Geist is my favorite teacher. I salute her brave commitment to her causes—and she has as many as I have designer outfits. But while she's into fashionable causes like helping the world and its people, animals, insects, and invertebrates and stuff, she's hugely fashionally challenged. Because of my respect for her, I've made it my personal cause to guide her into a more acceptable sartorial zone. We were making furious progress, too, but ever since she married Mr. Hall, our debate teacher, she's fallen off the fashion wagon. For some reason, marriage has made her less concerned about her appearance than ever. It makes my job even more of a challenge, but I totally live for challenges.

Realizing she had as much cooperation as could reasonably be expected, Miss Geist began. "Today we're starting a new unit, titled 'The Environment and You.' Open your books to page seventy-six."

Geist was riveted to her teacher textbook. Which is why she didn't see my hand in the air right away. But when she looked up, she acknowledged me immediately.

"Yes, Cher? You have a question already? We haven't started yet."

"Not exactly a question, Miss Geist. More of a suggestion."

She looked puzzled.

"That shift you have on?" I continued. "With all due respect, it totally begs for a jacket with clean, functional lines. I have one in my locker. May I get it for you?"

"That's very thoughtful of you, Cher, dear, but maybe later. We have important ground to cover here. Class?" Miss Geist went back to the text.

De tapped me on the back. "You nailed it with the

jacket, girlfriend. Like, hello? You'd think she'd jump at the chance at couture improvement. Does marriage make you oblivious or something?"

Amber, sitting next to me, chimed in with her opinion. "Maybe she's just so ecstatic with her new life as Mrs. Hall, she thinks she's the bomb even when she's viciously mismatched."

De and I laughed loudly. "Another subject on which Amber rules."

"Face it, Geist has the man of her dreams"—Amber was getting into dramatic: her specialty—"and he thinks she's beautiful no matter what she's wearing. And that's enough for her."

"Hello? If the man of my dreams didn't care what I looked like, I'd suspect he was dreaming about someone else," De said decisively, casting a suspicious eye at the back of the room, where Murray was playing a video game on his PowerBook.

"How you look is a reflection of how you feel, Amber," I said. Then I glanced at her ensemble-du-ridiculous and added, "By that estimation, I'd say the couture fairy was a little out of sorts this morning?"

"Excuse me, your fashion eminence, may I remind you that we are wearing fishnets over tights, now—"

"But *we* are not wearing them in last semester's hues," De pointed out.

We were so busy trading one-ups, we barely noticed that Geist's lesson had come to an abrupt halt. This time it was due to the intrusion of an outsider who'd slipped into the classroom and was at this moment handing several sheets of paper over to our teacher.

De, Amber, and I paused to assess. The outsider was definitely not part of our popular crowd. But her solid rep preceded her: Mackenzie Collins, granola girl. Mack, like Miss Geist, was all cause and no couture. But unlike Geist, it wasn't due to cluelessness or lack of resources. Mackenzie's family owned several Lexus dealerships around town, but she'd like made this personal choice to ride a bike to school. And it wasn't even a Peugeot.

Mackenzie, who totally towered over tiny Geist, was explaining, "This just came by fax to the office while I was on monitor duty. Vice Principal Gardner asked me to deliver it right away."

"What would you call that style she's wearing?" De asked, noting Mack's generic overalls, flannel shirt, and rugged yet tattered Earth shoes.

"House of No Style?" I guessed, calculating that if Mackenzie just replaced the flannel with a crop T— either Agnès B. or Max Azria—one vast stride toward a fashion statement would be taken.

De mused, "She's got good hair, but it screams for a stylist."

Mack had shiny ginger locks that cascaded to her waist in symmetrical waves. I added, "And her skin is flawless, but without contouring and shading, she just looks pale."

De nodded. "As I see it, the problem is, she's not saying anything with her look. Even grunge, retro as it is, would be a statement."

"Solid, De, but grunge is about angst. The word on Mackenzie is that she's not into the whole Courtney Love angst trip. She's more like a green zealot."

"She's the Green Hornet?" Amber, momentarily hearing-impaired due to Jesse Fiegenhut slipping his Discman earphones over her head, leaned over to ask.

De tried to swallow what would have been an embarrassingly loud laugh, so what she said came out more as a snort. "No, Ambu-lamebrain, Cher said zealot, not hornet! Mackenzie's some kind of ecology maven. Like to her, green is a way of life, not the hot shade of this year's Galliano line."

Amber seemed to get it. "Eeeww," she opined, scrunching up her surgically correct nose. "Like those losers who think plants and packaging rule over popularity and fashion?"

I didn't get further into it, because it suddenly hit me that Mackenzie reminded me of someone, only I couldn't figure out who. Then I realized—doy—she totally gives off the same aura as my ex-stepbrother, Josh, current college student and original cause-boy. Mackenzie Collins was like his female equivalent.

"Thank you, Mackenzie," Miss Geist was saying with an almost wistful smile as the Greenpeace poster child left our room. Geist clearly had a soft spot for Mack. The survey said: the daughter she never had.

As our teacher eyeballed the multipaged fax, this humongo smile sailed across her face. "Look, class, this fits in with our lesson!" Geist said almost giddily. "How perfect."

Since most of the class couldn't remember what the lesson was, the perfection was massively lost on us. But Geist's voice was sure and steady as she scanned and explained. "This is an announcement for an Environmental Challenge. It says that Bronson Alcott High School is invited to participate in a districtwide competition. Students must create a proactive environmental project or plan, and the school with the best one wins."

"You mean like a science project, but without the science?" I guessed.

Geist looked up. "Well, that's one way to look at it, Cher. Oh, and look. They even give suggestions for the projects. Let's see what they have here," she said, running her finger down the list of ideas. "Water conservation, um, that's a good one. . . . Recycling, yes, very important, air pollution, definitely, and, oh! my favorite, the rain forest . . ." As Geist read on, she was getting more pumped with each eco-suggestion, so excited that she didn't notice when one piece of paper flew out of her hands and glided to the floor. Where it would have stayed, happily ignored, if the class brownnose, Janet Hong, hadn't rushed from her seat to pick it up.

"Here, Miss Geist, you dropped this."

"Thank you, Janet," Geist said, turning her attention to the flyaway sheet. Then her forehead wrinkled and she frowned slightly. "Did this come with the notice about the Environmental Challenge? I can't imagine . . . it's something about, I suppose this is a new coffee shop . . . the Fashion Café? This must have gotten mixed up with the Environmental Challenge announcement by mistake. I'm sure there's no connection between . . ."

Okay, so I may not be an enviro-head, but I do know something about the Fashion Café. Far, far—nay, *galaxies*—from a mere coffee shop, it's a total historical hybrid: a museum of fashion, supermodels, and nouvelle cuisine. And at that second I'd have been willing to bet my new Badgley Mischka—okay, maybe the Dolce & Gabbana—that nothing less than fate had brought that Fashion Café fax into our sophomore social studies class. Call me mental, but I had this weird feeling there so *was* a connection between it and that enviro-challenge thing. A connection that would be lost without swift and immediate intervention. For the third time that period, a record, as De would point out later, my arm shot into the air.

7

"No, Cher, not now." Geist was getting a little testy with me. "We'll discuss your jacket later."

"Excuse me, it's not about that, Miss Geist. With all due respect, could you read that part about the Fashion Café again? It came with the Environmental Challenge announcement, and I have a feeling there is a connection here. And I know I speak for the entire class when I say we're massively interested in *everything* to do with the environment."

Geist looked a little dubious but shrugged her shoulders and agreed to read. And that's when she uttered the magic words.

"It seems that Cher is correct. I don't understand it, but it appears as if the Environmental Challenge is, in fact, sponsored by . . . the Fashion Café." Geist looked up. "I've never heard of it—has anyone else?" Thirty pairs of hands flew into the air—even Janet Hong's.

"It says," Geist reluctantly continued, "that a branch of the internationally famous Fashion Café is opening here in Beverly Hills. Because the opening coincides with Earth Day, they're inviting all the high schools in the district to submit projects relating to the environment. Judges from the café will then choose the best project. Representatives from the winning high school will attend the Fashion Café's opening night."

The worshipful silence that filled our classroom must have stunned Miss Geist because she looked up and paused before continuing. "And additionally, the winning high school will be awarded its own permanent display case, mounted on the wall of the Fashion Café's new Beverly Hills branch."

Everything was a blur after that. I vaguely remember Geist valiantly trying to remind us that "what's important here is not that Fashion Café part. What's important is that this challenge gives Bronson Alcott High School an opportunity to get involved, to display our creativity, and to show the world that our hearts, minds, and souls are truly committed to a cleaner planet, a healthier environment . . ."

De, Amber, and I turned solemnly to one another. Like who would not agree about the rampant significance of the environment and all? But the Fashion Café—*not* the important part? Hello? It was the mother ship calling us home.

Chapter 2

We weren't the only students so deeply affected by the announcement, which Mackenzie had judiciously distributed around the school. By lunch period the Quad, our lushly landscaped and terraced outdoor dining area, was ablaze with activity and buzz.

"I haven't seen this much school spirit since they installed those cappuccino-dispensing vending machines," I observed to De and Amber.

"Or when they agreed to provide valet parking in Student Lot B for the influx of luxury vehicles," De added.

De, Amber, and I expertly balanced our lunch trays, cellulars, and backpacks and strode over to meet our friends at our reserved table. Because we comprise the most envied crowd, which includes the Crew—the only crushworthy boys here on planet High School—we occupy the table with the primo location. It overlooks gushing fountains and features natural breezes, compliments of sculpted palm trees and Santa Ana winds. As we walked, every conversation pit we passed was animatedly discussing the grand opening of the Fashion Café.

We couldn't help overhearing soupçons of random conversation.

"The Fashion Café! I saw it on E! It's way cool, a total fashion environment. It's like the Planet Hollywood of the fashion world. . . ."

And "I've got a video of it. You should see the waiters—they strut the catwalk after they take your order. They are so doable!"

And reverentially, "It was created by the founding supermodels of our planet—Claudia, Elle, Naomi, and Christy."

And "My cousin's going to the one in New Orleans, and I'm like, 'Get me a leather jacket with the logo!'"

And then, as we settled into our table, there was this one from our own corner of the Quad. It was courtesy of Amber and delivered in hushed, dramatic tones suitable for the subject. "I was there."

De and I eyeballed her suspiciously. "Like, where, Amber? Where were you?"

Amber looked furtively around before answering, as if eavesdroppers who might give away the new Todd Oldham line were hiding in the shrubbery. "Remember our last school hiatus? When you guys went to Baja? Anyone remember why I didn't go with you?"

"Because we didn't invite you?" De guessed.

Excuse me, Dionne," Amber said. "I don't have to be invited. It's assumed I'm invited. Anyway, I didn't go because I had, like, a better offer."

When we didn't respond, she continued. "I went to New York. You must remember how I came back with the new DKNY before it was available in LA? I was like, the first to have it? And how some people at this very table were *très* jealous?"

My only memory was that she'd paired her DKNY tweed-and-lace look with an acid Betsey Johnson, totally ruining her couture coup. Totally Amber.

"Anyway," she continued, "while in Nueva Yorka, I had the opportunity to tour the actual Fashion Café. I, Amber Salk, was there."

I'm not sure what reaction Amber, like, expected from us. The only one she got was from Tai Fraser, the junior associate member of our crowd, who said slowly, "Wow, Amber. You were there."

But that was enough for Ambu-larity, who now had the floor and wasn't about to cede before declaring, "We must enter this competition! We must—and we will—win this competition! Girlfriends, this is the most important event in our nascent young lives! We will be encased, englassed, enclosed in perpetuity behind bulletproof glass, on the famed walls next to"—and here Amber had to take a deep breath—"Versace's display of the gold aluminum dress worn by Claudia . . . Armani's black-and-gold-sequined pantsuit worn by Jodie Foster . . . the Gaultier bustier Madonna wore in her Blonde Ambition tour . . ."

Amber's enthusiasm was majorly catching. And it was spreading around our table like that Ebola virus. As pumped as I'd been just hearing the announcement in class, well, like cube that now. Ditto for De, who got so excited whirling around to me, she accidentally flipped over her lunch tray, sending her croissant-wich flying across the table.

"Did you hear her, Cher? We'll have a place on the Fashion Café's Wall of Fame and . . ."

I finished De's thought, as I so often do. ". . . we'll be rubbing buffed elbows with supermodel-slash-moguls, parading down the catwalk that leads to our exhibit. Tourists will flock to see it! Is this not the quintessential us?"

De was all, "Okay, so at the opening, I'll wear the Vivienne Westwood. . . ."

"I'm totally thinking this event calls for that new crimson Alaïa halter dress I saw in the window on Rodeo. After all, you have to consider how we'll look in *People* magazine's 'Star Tracks' column. One should always be immortalized in one's best seasonal colors, and, De, you're a total winter."

De and I were furiously high-fiving each other when Amber broke in with a pronouncement. It rubbed us the way a Calvin in the irregular bin might. It was something like "And I, Amber Salk, will lead us to victory on this project."

Like, what? Amber lead us? How oxymoronic can you get? Or even just plain moronic.

"Excuse me, Major General Salk," I interrupted. "Either I missed the ballot-stuffing or something, but exactly when did *you* get elected queen of the Fashion Café project?"

Amber gave me one of her patented squinty-eyed looks. "Excuse *me*, your Cher-and-mightyness, but by process of elimination, I am the only one remotely capable of leading us to victory."

I was so stunned by her hubris, I didn't even respond. So De did.

"Only if those *Independence Day* aliens invaded would you be the one left to lead us to victory. And even then I'd demand a recount!"

"My woman speaks the truth," said Murray, who,

along with Sean, had just joined us and had no clue what De was even talking about. Still, I applauded his support. Even if it did elicit the frosty "Do not objectify me" response we've all come to expect from De. It's one in a series of way public spats and spills De and Murray indulge in daily. If relationships came in ice-cream flavors, they'd be rocky road.

Amber ignored De and Murray, and started to list what she considered her qualifications. "First of all, as I've already mentioned, I'm the only one at this table who has been there."

"Color me excited," De deadpanned. "What else?"

"Excuse me, it's obvious. I'm the least ecologically challenged of anyone here."

"How you figure that?" Sean interjected.

"Maybe it's her aerodynamic hairdo," I ventured. "Environmentally sound but screamingly last period."

Amber viciously ignored us, which allowed me to remind everyone, "When it comes to leadership capabilities, I think we're all in agreement"—I glanced around the table for support—"that I totally excel in that area. Besides, Amber, was it not me who went on a wholly ecological nature retreat and organized an entire toxic cleanup crew? And was it not me who led the City Beautification effort and transformed that nasty lot into a park? I believe that totally qualifies me to lead this effort."

De seconded. "Cher's the diva of delegation. She even has awards for it." De was referring to the leadership award I'd recently received on the nature retreat.

Amber waved us away. "Jurassic news, girlfriends. That was then. This is now. And what qualifies *moi* is that I already have an idea for what our victorious project will be."

The project? What project? Oops, my bad. In all the hoopla about leadership skills and tourists flocking to our exhibit, I momentarily misplaced the notion about that science project part. And Amber already had an idea?

"Okay, Amber, chomp, chomp. I'll bite. Describe," I said coolly.

"A video!" she triumphantly declared. "A state of the art, cutting edge, caught-on-tape exposé!"

Tai was intrigued. "Like on *Hard Copy?* But who are we exposing?"

"Not who, *what,*" Amber said dramatically. "It's so simple, *mes amies,* it's classic. We'll use our video expertise to expose gross examples of the toxins that poison our planet right here at our very own stomping grounds."

"We have toxins stomping here?" Tai was genuinely surprised.

"Excuse me, just look around. What evils cloud your field of vision?"

We all looked, but all we saw was, duh, the Quad. Palm trees ringed by highly polished statues, marble water fountains, stone benches, demi-cliques of students representing our varied ethnicities, fringed by random co-minglers. Not a toxin in sight—unless you counted the sludge that was Amber's outfit.

Amber was all, do I have to draw you a picture? "That juice box!" She pointed accusingly at the one at Sean's lips. "Do you even know what kind of planetary havoc it wreaks?"

Startled, Sean squeezed it too hard, spraying the artsy member of our clique, Summer, who screamed at him.

"And where, I demand to know," Amber continued, "are the outdoor recycling bins? Must we continue to bear the burden of toting our recyclables all the way back inside the commissary? And has anyone checked to see that those fountains get shut off once we are back in the building? And our textbooks—are they made from recycled paper? I think not!"

I could see where she was going with this. Amber had a killer point—several in fact, even apart from her last-season, pointy-toed Joan & David's. There totally were gross examples of planetary waste right here on our hallowed turf. Which, now pointed out, did not go unappreciated by members of our *déjeuner* posse. They hastily climbed aboard the Amber bandwagon.

"Monster idea, Amber!" Tai, all wide-eyed, said.

"Like totally cool." Jackson Doyle, our token slacker, slid in next to Tai and roused his brain cells to form a thought.

"Yo, I could get behind that." Sean actually seemed thoughtful as he stared hypnotically at his squished juice box. Amber looked grievously pleased with herself.

But there was something about Amber's vicious exposé idea, worthy though it might be, that just didn't fall in the right places for me. Like when shoulder pads extend that quarter inch too far out. So when she turned to me, victory flashing in her sharp eyes, as Amber herself would say, I just had to be honest.

"While I totally agree about the rampant waste here, the whole concept of an exposé is so . . . negative. I make a motion that we not rush into anything and focus our creativity on developing a project with a more positive spin on it. Who seconds?"

"I do. Cher excels at accentuating the positive," chimed in a distinctly male and familiarly smarmy voice. New county heard from as the slick and self-centered Jesse Fiegenhut insinuated himself into our party. Jesse was a major Baldwin, the undisputed leader of the Crew, and ridiculously rich. The one thing he couldn't buy was the concept that I am not, nor will ever be, attracted to him.

"Accentuate whatever you want, Cher, especially those touch-up-impaired streaks of yours," Amber parried, "but allow *me* to be honest. *This* is the winning project. You'll just have to decide how badly you want to win this competition. Besides, once we air our exposé, the proper positive policy changes will no doubt ensue."

De, who had yet to commit, was getting swayed. "Amber might be making sense, Cher." It surprised me that De could use the words *Amber* and *sense* in the same sentence.

Then Amber turned to me with what had to be her snarkiest look all day.

"Your disagreeing wouldn't have anything to do with the stubborn refusal to admit that I have the better— oh, wait a minute, isn't it the *only*—idea here? You, Cher Horowitz, wouldn't possibly be putting your own petty competition with *moi*, Amber Salk, ahead of the good of all of us, would you?"

"As if!" I sniffed. "I'm not stubborn! Besides, can't I just dislike your idea without any personal vendetta?"

"Cher would never put her personal feelings ahead of the greater good," De added, swinging over quickly to my defense.

"Yeah, Cher's fair," Murray said.

"The fairest of them all," Jesse added with a wink. Which I ignored. I turned to Murray. "So you agree with me, Murray? That we should come up with a more tasteful, less tabloidy project?"

I don't know why, but at that moment I felt the burning need for an ally. But I didn't get support from

Murray—at least not right away. Instead, Murray was all, "Yo, I got my own problems with this whole gig. Like, what's in it for the brothers? Why should we be down with this girlie-girl Fashion Cafeteria scene?"

It shocked me that no one had a rejoinder. Sean, Jesse, and even Jackson suddenly seemed to wonder the same thing. So I jumped in. "Well, okay, you don't *have* to be involved. I'm sure the Fashion Café's Environmental Challenge isn't mandatory." I winked at De and continued. "So when *we* attend opening night, you'll just have to tell us which supermodels—Naomi, Claudia, Elle, or Christy—you brothers want autographs from."

Murray's eyes got wider than a plus-size dress from the Richard Simmons collection. "Those supermodel babes are gonna be there?"

"Well, duh, Murray, do they not own the Fashion Café? Would they have, like, something better to do on opening night?"

"Put your tongue back in your mouth, slobber-boy, you're drooling," De said.

"So what are we waitin' for? Let's move to the project groove." Murray practically bolted from his seat as he turned to me. "If Amber's *Hard Copy*-inspired, trash-trawling approach doesn't float your boat, let's get busy."

Before I could respond, Sean interrupted. "Chill, bro, I'm down with Amber's videology thing. What you got against it anyway?"

Murray looked puzzled until De elbowed him and answered, "Too much is at stake here to blindly rush into the first idea that comes up. Let's give it a little thought like Cher says."

"I'm thinkin', woman, I'm thinkin' real hard," Murray said with a furious, all-braces-baring smile.

As the debate raged around me, I realized Murray had nailed it. Some furiously serious thinking had to ensue. If I didn't want to climb aboard the Amber-exposé express, I had to think of something else. Something that would totally lead me and my t.b.'s to fame and glory in the Fashion Café.

Chapter 3

I live in a chronic Beverly Hills villa. It's architecturally enhanced with lush landscaping, plush decor, flushly accessorized with a clay tennis court, kidney-shaped pool, and backyard putting green. Thanks to my careful management and eye for detail, our home is an oasis of taste in a nabe too often riddled with gigabits of ostentatious vulgarity.

As I entered our dramatic, vaulted-ceilinged foyer, I heard the familiar symphony of multiphone lines ringing, fax machines spewing, fingers clack-clacking on keyboards, and modems squawking.

It was all punctuated with barks of "Get me that depo now!" And "No, I will not speak with Hummelberger!" And "Who's the knucklehead who came up with the idea to quash that motion?" And finally "Cher! Is that you?"

"Your favorite daughter, Daddy," I said, swinging into his palatial study. I stood on the tiptoes of my ankle-strapped Miu Miu platforms to plant a wet one on his cheek.

"My only daughter, as I recall," Daddy faux-gruffly acknowledged.

Since my mom died when I was still in designer diapers, and I'm sibling challenged—in the biological sense, which does not include Josh—Daddy and I mainly live here alone. But we're never lonely. We're host to a bodacious roster of household help. Lucy, our housekeeper, Rico, our gardener, and José, on pool patrol, are major domos of their own mini-staffs.

Daddy's the most fearsome litigator in all of Beverly Hills. He and I have this unspoken deal. I'm in charge of his nutritional and sartorial needs. He's in charge of my charges, as in plastic. No matter how busy we are, we always make quality time for each other. I told Daddy all about the fabulous new challenge in my life.

"All I need to do is come up with a killer environmental project, and my t.b.'s and I will have achieved fashion immortality. All before our sixteenth birthdays. Pretty groovy, huh, Daddy?" Though it's not my habit to indulge in sixties jargon, I find myself lapsing into it around Daddy occasionally.

To my rampant chagrin, Daddy didn't seem pumped about my new challenge. Instead of saying as he usually does, "What's this going to cost me, Cher?" he was all in harrumph mode.

"The environment! Another of those nineties inventions. Back in the sixties we had real causes—civil rights, we marched on Washington, we . . ."

Okay, so Daddy keeps forgetting that it was Uncle Marvin and not him actually present at the marches, still I knew what was coming next. So before Daddy launched into one of his "Hey, hey, LBJ" chants, I gently reminded him that it wasn't just the environment at stake here: it was the Fashion Café. But once Daddy latches on to a theme, it's hard to, like, get him to brake for animals. He was all, "I've litigated cases against some of these nut jobs, who've taken this hooey too far. Some of them want to eliminate all off-shore drilling, and because of one drunken sailor, Exxon got stuck with a bill for millions."

"But, Daddy," I protested, looking at his secretary for what little reinforcement I might get, "what about that Rendezvous cruise line that's been all over the MTV news lately? Aren't they like pouring toxic sludge into the ocean?"

"It's more complicated than that, Cher. It has to do with the laws about waste disposal of by-products." Just then Daddy's secretary interrupted that Magistrate O'Halloran was still holding. Daddy shook his finger at me and added, "Just remember, nothing's black and white. There are two sides to everything, not counting the loopholes."

I took a deep breath and reassessed. This environmental stuff might be more complicated than originally anticipated. I slinked out of Daddy's office, whipped out my cellular, and speed-dialed De.

"Zup, girlfriend?" she answered after only half a ring.

"De, we've so totally got to come up with something environmentally proper. If not, we're stuck with Ambu-lame's idea. And it isn't because of any personal sense of competition. Really, De, you know me better than anyone, and even if Amber is a jagged little pill, she is our jagged little pill."

"Every posse's gotta have one," De agreed.

"So it's not that. I just think—I know!—we can do better."

"Solid, Cher. I'm there. What's our next step?"

"I can't be certain. But I think we should take it at the mall . . . okay?"

"After school tomorrow, girlfriend, done deal."

Later, when Lucy buzzed upstairs to tell me dinner was ready, I'd showered, changed, and was feeling way confident. A mood that got almost immediately smashed by the surprise appearance of a third setting at our dinner table.

It wasn't the placement of silverware and Limoges that blitzed my good-mood bubble. Instead, it was the life-form perched on the chair in front of it. Josh had this amazing ability to show up just as food was about to hit the table. His flanneled back was to me as I strode into the dining room. I was just about to deliver a dazzling display of put-downism at its finest, when it suddenly hit me.

Hello? Like, anybody there, Cher? Am I not in need of a monster enviro-project? Do I not have the prince of enviro-boys right here, at my doorstep, at my dinner table, at my—if I play my cards right—beck and call?

"Josh!" I burbled. "I am so massively psyched to see you!" To punctuate, I dropped a tiny peck on the top of his head before prancing to my seat.

"What do you want, Cher." It was a statement rather than a question, delivered between slurps of gazpacho soup, which he hadn't even politely waited for me to start.

I gave him my best wide-eyed mock innocence. "Why do I have to want something? Can't I just be pumped to see you? My authentically faux ex-stepbrother, who honors us with his presence way too sporadically?" Carefully I picked up my napkin and placed it in my lap.

Daddy was on his cellular and waved at me to start eating.

"Like I said, Cher, what's up? You are never happy to see me, let alone pumped, psyched, or, let's see . . . what's that other patented Cherism? Viciously thrilled? So what is it this time? Wait, let me guess. You need a ride somewhere. Have the taxis to the Galleria gone on strike? Or did they eliminate valet parking at the Beverly Center?"

I was tempted to go tease for taunt. But then I stopped. The history between me and Josh was, to say the least, fractious. As in, Josh and I generally snipe at each other from soup to tiramisu. A tactic, based on current circumstances, that seemed less than practical.

So I looked into Josh's canny but cloudless baby blues and went minimalist. "I need a cause."

Josh was majorly blasé, as if random streetpeople said this to him all the time.

"You need a cause," he echoed. Then he put down his soup spoon and slid into a snipe-fest. "What's wrong with the normal causes in the land of superficial reality? Isn't working on your body, your clothes, your hair, your nails, and your popularity fulfilling enough?"

To my immense credit, I did not take the bait. I simply explained, "My t.b.'s and I have decided to use our popularity for a good, earth-enhancing cause. I just need some input on what the lucky cause will be, and who better to mentor us than you? Aren't you saving yourself for a career in environmental law? We just want a cause that will help the environment."

I thought that sounded way convincing, but not to Josh. He was all, "Where have I heard this before? Every time you decide to use your popularity for a good cause, there's usually some big selfish payoff for you.

So what is it this time, Cher? Negotiating for an A in social studies?"

"I never realized what a skeptic you've become, Josh. Can't I just be altruistic?"

"No, Cher, you can't."

We'd gotten through both soup and salad—which Daddy, still on the cell, had pushed away. We were ready for our chicken marsala, and I hadn't made any progress with Josh. So I came clean with him. I explained about our school's Environmental Challenge in great depth, and then, at the very end, tossed in the part about the Fashion Café and the supermodels who thought of it.

Understanding filled Josh's eyes.

Cynicism tinged his voice.

"Supermodels. Those semistarved symbols of superficiality are sponsoring an environmental challenge. That proves it. The apocalypse *has* arrived."

I let Josh rant.

"Explain the connection to me. What is fashion's sudden fascination with the environment?"

"Tscha, Josh! You're using the narrowest definition of fashion. It's not just about clothes and supermodels. It's way fashionable to want a clean planet. And I totally support that."

Josh was silent for a moment. Then he said, "Your logic stuns me."

"So that means you'll help?"

"No way."

"Come on, Josh. I know that deep in that college-boy heart of yours you're dying to help me become a better person; more environmentally enhanced. Like you're always parading around with these T-shirt sayings. Let's see, what is it today?"

I gently parted Josh's flannel to expose his PC T-shirt du jour. It read Support the People of the Rain Forest.

"See, I believe in that," I said. "I think we should be majorly supportive of others. But exactly what do they need? A twelve-step program?"

"Don't even start, Cher," Josh said.

I gave him my sweetest pleading look.

Josh sighed. "Okay, Cher. It refers to stopping the plunder of our rain forests and allowing the indigenous people to live there in peace."

"I'm in total agreement that the indigents should have a place to stay. It's part of that food, clothing, shelter thing. But why relegate them only to the rain forest? We have excellent accommodations in many other sunnier places."

Josh rolled his eyes. "Indigenous people, Cher, not indigent. It refers to the people who have lived in harmony with their fragile and rapidly disappearing environment for centuries. It means that they belong there."

"Kind of like how I belong in Beverly Hills?" I piped up.

Josh grinned. "Not kind of, Cher. Exactly. For once, you've got it exactly right."

"So now you'll help?" I asked.

"I'll think about it, Cher."

At school the next day we were summoned into an assembly. Topic: the Fashion Café. As it pertains to the Environmental Challenge.

I had to give snaps to the administration for their prompt attention to detail regarding this way important development in our studies. They'd totally caucused and come up with the school rules regarding the competition.

Miss Geist was in charge. Standing on a step stool so she could be seen over the podium, she nudged her slippery glasses up on her nose and explained, "As you are aware, our school has been invited to participate in an exciting new project, the Environmental Challenge. Because Bronson Alcott High School is committed to this most pressing cause, we will accept the invitation, but . . ."

De turned to me. "Whenever she says 'but,' we've got complications."

"Nothing we can't handle," I assured her.

Miss Geist continued. "We want to be sure that students aren't becoming involved simply because of the Fashion Café. We want to see a real commitment to the environment. Therefore, we, your teachers and administrators, have added our own challenge."

Geist scanned the auditorium. Not a cellular in sight. She had the significant attention of all the students. She smiled and went on. "For the first part of the competition, teams of students are invited to submit written outlines for an Environmental Challenge project. We, the teachers"—Geist turned to acknowledge her peer group, seated in folding chairs behind her on the stage—"will grade them based on merit."

An arm shot up from the center of the auditorium. "Does spelling count?"

Geist ignored the interruption. "We will then choose the most merit-worthy idea from each grade, one each from our seniors, juniors, sophomores, and freshmen. That will net us four teams of semifinalists. Those four teams will get the go-ahead to pursue their projects with the help of a faculty adviser. The completed projects will then be presented at our school's very first Environmental Expo. There a panel of judges will award points to each one."

I turned to De. "No problem." She high-fived me. Geist, of course, wasn't finished.

"But the presentation only counts for fifty percent of the grade. There is another element to the challenge which will count for another fifty percent. Winners will be chosen not only on their projects, but on what they, as a team, have done individually to help the environment."

A collective gasp reverberated throughout the auditorium.

Geist didn't falter. "For example, if you submit an idea for a waste disposal system and it is chosen as a semifinalist, in order to win, you must also show how you have taken positive steps toward a cleaner planet. We want a pledge from each student involved in this challenge. So"—she took a breath—"to recap: fifty percent of your grade will be based upon your execution of the project—how merit-worthy and compelling it is. The other fifty percent will be based on what each member of your team has done personally to support the cause. Whichever team has the most points will represent Bronson Alcott in the Environmental Challenge."

Geist wrapped by saying that our submissions had to be in by the end of the week.

As we filed out of the auditorium, Amber was in a huff. "Excuse me, how fair is that? The Fashion Café didn't ask for a personal commitment, just a project. Why should we have to do extra credit?"

De was philosophical. "Don't get your follicles in a

frenzy, Amber. It makes chronic sense that the teachers would come up with this. They don't feel they're doing their job unless they add input. Or are you not up to the new challenge?"

"As if!" Amber sniffed.

I added, "Personally, I give snaps to the teachers. It gives us the opportunity to be fully innovative and focus on more than one environmental injustice at the same time. I, for one, can't wait to get started."

"You do that, Cher," Amber said, turning on her chunky heel. "I already am started." She flounced toward her next class.

Chapter 4

*A*fter school De and I did mall time. Because the goal of our journey was not solely acquisitive but inspiration-seeking, we chose BeachSide Mall. What it lacked in a food court and a plethora of important designers, it made up for in its proximity to our ecologically impaired waterfront. It also featured chronic retail outlets like Contempo Casuals and Wet Seal.

We'd barely taken three baby steps into the latter when De's cellular rang. She rolled her eyes—it had to be Murray. He was always beeping her whenever she was out of flying paper-missile range. He totally put the capital *P* on *Possessive*. While De riffed with Murray, I started power-shopping, waiting for inspiration to hit.

While I wasn't counting on finding much that was majorly plastic-worthy at BeachSide, I did surprise myself by managing to fill up several shopping bags in a relatively short span. A total must-have sleeveless shantung Cynthia Rowley and the actual shade of pearlized vermilion sandals that Neiman's had been out of. Nylon platform joggers by Pom D'Api and Rusted Rose Hard Candy nail polish.

Between Murray-beeps, De filled some holes in her wardrobe, too. She found a Gaultier scarf that went with her golden new shift, and a Calvin lasso belt that would be outstanding with her midriff-baring Gucci hiphuggers.

I checked my Movado. Time on task: two hours. We had stuff, but so far? No eco-ideas. Whenever shopping didn't work by itself, the best accessory was an ingestive sidebar.

"Let's go upload a cappuccino," I suggested.

De flipped her cellular and called ahead to reserve a table at the freestanding Starbucks exhibit on the upper level.

As we sat down to our double decaf lattes, we surveyed our surroundings. We hadn't done this level yet, and that new expanded Victoria's Secret had definite possibilities. Which I was just about to mention to De when I saw something rampantly jarring.

"De, check it, at three o'clock. Talk about someone nonindigenous to her environment!"

De peered over her latte to where I was pointing.

It was . . . Mackenzie Collins? She was with other members of her trail-mix posse, including Ariel Milano, Shawna Stern, and that girl who kept changing her name from Melissa to Clarissa and back. Decked out in denim-du-jour and untucked flannel, they were grossly underaccessorized. Mack, Ariel, and Melissa-Clarissa came equipped only with canvas fanny packs, barely roomy enough for a wallet, let alone makeup, compact, and cellular. Only Shawna carried a full-size bag. It was a tote. But instead of a designer logo, it was stamped with the slogan Think Globally, Act Locally.

"I wonder what they're doing here?" I mused. "Don't tell me the green-gang girls are closet mall-hoppers?"

"Not even," De replied. "I bet they go into that vintage clothing store."

I stood up for a better view. "Good guess, girlfriend," I acknowledged. "They're just turning into Second Hand Rose."

And as they disappeared into the most skippable store in the mall, it hit me—with a tsunami force so gigantic, it nearly knocked me over on my four-inch platforms. The idea we'd come to find was right here waiting for us—in our own indigenous environment.

"That's it! De, girlfriend! I've so totally got it! I just put it all together!" In my pumped-up stage, I hadn't even noticed that De was on the phone yet again with Murray. She paused.

"Hold on a sec, Murray. Cher's got something. . . . No, it isn't catching. Hold on."

I burst out with, "Okay, so like, the tote Mackenzie's friend was carrying . . ."

De was puzzled. "Her tote? What about it?"

"It said Think Globally. . . ."

"And?"

"I'm totally thinking globally: Versace—Italian; Gaultier—French; Kenzo—Asian; Lagerfeld—German; Calvin—American . . . this is so dope!"

De was lost, so I breathlessly connected the dots.

"Okay, so now Act Locally. What does that mean, De? Look around at our locale. Where are we?"

"BeachSide Mall?" she guessed.

"No, not literally at this second. I meant our total environment. Is Beverly Hills not the fashionable capital of the world? Use your accessory-ability and put it all together. Does it not so scream 'fashion show'? That's what our project will be. A fashion show. I've been to so many with Daddy for all his major disease benefits, I could organize it in my sleep. It's way indigenous."

De was listening to me and explaining to Murray at the same time, "Cher's idea for our project is a fashion show."

She turned to me. "Murray's like, 'What does that have to do with the environment?'"

"That's the most chronic part, De! Our fashions will all be made out of environmentally sound materials, i.e., recyclables." I could feel my eyes flashing and the hairs on the back of my neck standing at attention. Like when the one dress you *have* to have actually comes in your size. And in your color. And matches your car.

I was profoundly juiced. "This is so us! This is the total expression of who we are and what we can do for our planet. Hello? We are already committed to recycled stuff. I mean, we are—and I don't mean to be immodest—the total champions of plastic usage. And is plastic not the Dalai Lama of all recyclables?"

De was there. "You know, you're right, Cher. We *are* into all things plastic. Like who has not considered, if not already had, plastic surgery?"

I added, "And all forms of recycling, too. Look at your hair extensions—they're totally recycled from other people."

De was way into it now. "And are not divorced and remarried parents simply recycled parents?"

"That's what makes this idea so organic," I said triumphantly. "It's way indigenous to us. To who we are. In our—what did Josh say?—our fragile and something-or-other environment."

De was all, "So in our fashion show, we'll do recycled clothing? Like used stuff . . . in earth tones?" She glanced uncomfortably at Second Hand Rose.

"Not even, Dionne. Vintage clothing is an overexposed concept. Like those milk mustache commercials. Or Jenny McCarthy."

De giggled. "So what you had in mind was . . ."

"Fashion that is created from recycled products." I said that with major flourish. Even if, okay, I admit, I didn't know exactly what that could be. But I was so filled with confidence, I continued. "Our team will demonstrate the great melding of fashion and ecology. It's so synergistic—and choice! We'll not only trash Ambu-lame and her vicious exposé with an apt demonstration of solution-oriented positive energy, we'll win the grand prize."

"Oooh, sounds dope, Cher." De was pumped. "I can see us now, parading down the catwalk in our recyclables." She stopped for a sec, turned to her cellular, and then said, "Murray wants to know if we'll be modeling fashions made of peach pits?"

I rolled my eyes and grabbed the cell.

"Not biodegradable, Murray, recyclable! Like what exactly are recyclables we can wear? Well, duh, I haven't gotten to that part yet, but once we snag that semifinalist gig, we'll totally figure it out. You and De are with me, right?"

They were. De and I bounded out of BeachSide, shopping bags swinging in one hand, high-fiving each other with the other, all the way home.

All my buds were way into it, too. Everyone I called applauded my stroke of genius and were all like, "Sign me up, Cher. I'm on your team." That is, the ones

Amber hadn't already ensnared, like Tai, Sean, Jackson Doyle, and other easily led randoms. Whatever.

My team, Cher's Crewsaders, was A-list. I had De, I had Murray, I had Jesse, though that was always a borderline call. Plus, I had Summer and was pretty sure of Janet Hong, though she claimed she had to finish her honors algebra homework before she could commit. All I needed now was that go-ahead semifinalist award from Geist. I felt rampantly secure that we'd get it, too.

On the appointed afternoon, we filed into the auditorium to hear the announcements of the semifinalist winners. I'd never seen our school's auditorium so full. It was like an Oasis/Alanis double bill: way SRO. Geist and company were out in full force, lined up on the stage in metal folding chairs.

"Look at the cute faculty," De pointed out. "They're totally kvelling from one end of the stage to another." She was right. All our teachers were beaming. None more brightly than Geist, who stepped up to the podium, spread her notes in front of her, and began.

"Before we announce our semifinalists, I'd like to take a moment to congratulate all the students. I've never seen such an outpouring of ideas! You were all very creative and exceptionally motivated. Of course, it made our job very difficult, but after much discussion, we, the staff of Bronson Alcott High, have reached our decisions. Here are the teams who'll be pursuing their projects."

I waited for like, "The envelope, please," but Geist began the announcement *sans* accoutrements. De and I held hands in anticipation. I bit my lip.

"Representing the seniors, Courtney Barnes and Brianna Fuller will present an exhibition on beach erosion." A wild cheer went up from the senior section.

Courtney and Brianna were like the Cher and De of their class: the unchallenged leaders. Good choice, I thought. Our beaches were getting way eroded with generics. There was hardly any space left to catch decent rays.

"And representing our juniors," Geist announced as the senior cheers finally subsided, "is semifinalist Igor Azoff, whose team will tackle 'Pollution—Destiny or Chemistry?'" A polite smattering of applause greeted the choice. Igor was only peripherally known around the school. I couldn't imagine who'd be on his team or why he even cared about the Fashion Café. Still, I didn't want to be impolite, so I clapped.

De and I tightened our grip on each other as we were about to be crowned sophomore semifinalists. But to our major chagrin, Geist skipped right over us, going, "And the freshman semifinalists are Casey Johnson and Scott Berchman, who proposed 'Ten Energetic Ways to Save Energy.'"

Which didn't strike me as all that original, but what could you expect from freshmen? They were but tad-poles in the Alcott stream of life.

But why had Geist skipped the sophomores? Amber's arm flew into the air to ask precisely that, I was sure. But Geist shushed her.

"Some of you have obviously noticed that I didn't mention the sophomore winners. That's because we had the most difficult decision with that class. There were so many excellent ideas, we had an overabundance of riches. We couldn't single out just one. So, after much discussion and debate"—when she said the word "debate," she sneaked a glance at Mr. Hall, our debate teacher, and her husband, of course—"we picked two semifinalists from that class.

"So, to keep you in suspense no longer, our first sophomore winner is . . ."

I sucked in my breath. ". . . Cher's Crewsaders, led by Cher Horowitz, who will present 'Eco-High Fashion: Original, Indigenous, and Way Cutting Edge.'"

De and I bolted from our seats as Murray let out an ear-piercing whistle, pumping his arm to the "Whoo! Whoo! Whoo!" salute, which didn't seem nearly so juvenile just then. Thunderous applause broke out all over the room as De and I turned and waved to acknowledge our win.

"Settle down, students!" Mr. Hall stood up to lend support to his wife, who was having trouble controlling the outburst of support for our win. "Miss Geist has another name to read. Don't you, my dear?"

"Yes." She blushed. "Thank you. And our other sophomore semifinalist is . . ." I looked around and suddenly knew my ickiest fears were about to be confirmed. "Amber Salk, and her team, the, er, Amber's Angels, will present a video documentary, 'Toxins on Our Turf,' which will explore ways in which our own school environment can be improved ecologically."

Just then the chant, "Am-*ber!* Am-*ber!*" led by Sean and Tai, echoed around the room and took root as Amber grievously bowed to accept her due.

De and I were furiously chagrined.

"We were rooked! We had it way over her," De grumbled.

The assembly ended with Geist reminding us that the grand prize winner would be chosen based not only on the execution of the project itself, but on supporting data. "What each team member has done to personally pledge a commitment to the environment." She then gave us a deadline of three weeks from now and announced faculty advisers. Amber's team got Mr. Hall. We snared Geist herself.

"One up for us already," I said, winking at De and Murray. "Geist has way more credibility than anyone in the PC arena." Just as I said that, I wondered what Mackenzie Collins had submitted and why her team wasn't chosen. I scanned the auditorium for her, but the granola girls were Audi.

Chapter 5

I got home that day awash in high spirits. Even the sight of the step-drone splayed out on the couch in the den couldn't puncture my whimsically delirious mood.

Josh was reading something called *The Unbearable Lightness of Being*. The title struck me as unfinished. Like, *The Unbearable Lightness of Being* . . . who? Kate Moss? But I knew better than to ask and risk a put-down. So as I bounced onto the sectional next to him, I just said, "Hey, enviro-boy, guess what?"

"The shocking new Chanel came in your color?" he guessed.

"Don't be snide, Josh. In fact, it hasn't yet." I gave him a friendly little punch and said, "But something even better. My team is totally on its way to winning the Environmental Challenge. The faculty went for my idea of a fashion show with recyclables big time."

"Did they?" Josh didn't act as surprised as I thought

he might. "Looks like you don't need my help then." He went back to being unbearable. That is, reading it.

"*Au contraire,* Joshie. We still need to come up with personal pledges. And I'm so counting on you to help me come up with the unbearably winningest pledge," I said, with a nod at his reading matter.

Josh gave me a funny look that I later interpreted as faux annoyed. Like his brow kind of furrowed, yet he put down his book.

"Well, what is it exactly that you want to pledge yourself to, besides allegiance to the deity of vanity?"

Once again, I displayed a maturity way beyond my fifteen years. I did not return fire. I tossed back my shiny hair, turned to face Josh full on, and simply said, "Okay, look, I'm not exactly an environmental duh-head. I know the issues. But what would *you* consider, like, the top ten most pressing?"

Josh let out a long sigh. "Okay, Cher. What about pollution? You could do a report or something on it."

"You mean like smog?"

Then, I don't know why, maybe our big win had lowered my defenses, but I suddenly admitted to Josh, "When I was little, I used to think smog was like natural pollution. Like what Mother Nature wants us to have—otherwise, life in LA would be too majorly golden."

I immediately wished I hadn't opened up like that. I mentally ducked for Josh's snide comeback.

But it never came. Instead, Josh was all, "It's funny how we all make up stuff like that when we're younger. Unfortunately, we grow up and find out the bitter truth."

"Hmm," I agreed, "smog is a blight."

"So are car fumes. When cars burn gas, it's released into the air and results in acid rain. Why not pledge your commitment by riding a bike to school, Cher?"

"Hello? Have you ever tried pedaling in platforms? I don't think so." But as I said that, I totally flashed on Mackenzie Collins. "I need something more indigenous, Josh."

Just then my phone rang. "Keep thinking, bro," I said as I left the room to answer it.

Bro? When had I ever called Josh bro? This win had totally gone to my head. I fell asleep that night dreaming of the exact shade of the red carpet I'd be sashaying down on opening night—and what I could wear that wouldn't clash with it.

The next day in Hall's homeroom, I got a rude wake-up call: the frantically disturbing sight of Amber and her entire team—Sean, Tai, Jackson, Janet, who'd been swayed by Amber while doing her algebra assignment, and even the follicularly deprived Mr. Hall!—were all wearing deeply tacky pink T-shirts emblazoned with the logo Amber's Angels. They actually had halos over the A's. The leader of the tack-pack, Amber herself, was sporting two other accessories: a compact camcorder and a beret. She aimed one around the room haphazardly. The other balanced precariously on her hair-don't of the day.

De whistled under her breath. "She's got that director diva thing down already."

"Maybe," I sniffed, "but it's premature for Amy Heckerling to lose sleep. Besides, let Ambular have her fun. She with the most accoutrements doesn't always win. Her project is drowning in negativity, while ours

41

totally surfs with positive energy. On balance, she wipes out, we clean up."

In spite of my brave front, I was somewhat unnerved. Amber did seem to be ahead of us. Okay, we had our idea—but so far not the faintest way to implement it. As the bell rang for first period, I pulled De aside. "Meeting in study hall after fourth period—pass it on to our team." De duly whipped out her cellular and began the round of calls.

I spent my morning classes getting organized. In my capacity as Daddy's social secretary and his daughter, I developed the ability to concentrate on several things at once. So when Mrs. Hanratty, our algebra teacher, called on me to solve a complicated equation, I was able to deliver the right formula—x equals the sum of y squared—*and* write Jesse's name down as music coordinator on my fashion show master list at the same time. I had to be practical. What's a fashion show without music? And what else could I reasonably expect CD-head Jesse to do?

Jesse was way enthusiastic about the job I'd given him. So were my other Crewsaders, as I passed out assignments later in the study hall room.

"Okay, so the first convocation of Cher's Crewsaders will now come to order," I began, glancing meaningfully at my team. They respectfully wrapped their phoners to give me their undivided attention.

"The way I see this, the most important thing is to come up with the actual enviro-fashions."

"Well, duh, Cher, you just figure that out now?" Murray was totally being a wise guy. I suddenly realized how teachers like Geist and Hall must feel.

Summer chimed in with "Are we going to, like,

design our own fashions using milk jugs or something?"

"Um, good question, Summer," I responded. "I was
actually thinking that eco-clothes and accessories have
to exist somewhere. It'll be our mission to find them and
meld them into fashionable items. To that end, I'm
appointing De and Murray as co-CEOs of research,
cyber-department. You two will go on-line and see what
you can find."

De was all, "Proper. Fashion Web sites totally rule the
net. I'll surf tonight and make stops at all the majors."

"Exactly, Dionne," I agreed. "In my social studies
class this morning I had the opportunity to list a few.
Here are the Web addresses for Armani Exchange,
Nicole Miller, and Donna Karan. And don't forget generic
stops like the Fashion Net and Fashion Mall. But here," I
said, pushing my list in front of her. "There's also Diesel,
X-Girl, and Walter Van Beirendonck's Wild and Lethal
Trash."

De looked majorly dubious. "These are hardly majors,
Cher," she sniffed.

"That's my point, De. They may be just cutting edge
enough to delve into recyclables."

I eyeballed Murray. "Your mission—and with Naomi
and Claudia waiting, something tells me you'll accept
it—is to cyber-research on-line resources for generic
recyclables. We'll find a way to make them fashionable."

Murray peered at the labels of his Girbaud skate pants
and murmured, "Wonder what these are made of?"

I turned to Summer. "With your artistic flair, I'm
appointing you set designer."

"Cool, Cher. I'll head to Sam Flax after sixth period
and stock up on supplies," she responded.

"I got a question." Murray suddenly looked up from his label inspection. "While we're all doin' this, what exactly are you doing?"

"Doy, Murray, I'm team captain. I'm the delegator. And I'm totally in charge of putting this whole thing together. Which reminds me. There's something else I want to bring to the table."

Jesse looked around, expecting some take-out guy to pop in with snacks.

"Okay, so here's the thing. We are totally going to win, but I can't shake the feeling that there's something lacking on our team. Like a V-neck sweater without . . ."

". . . a Y necklace?" De guessed.

"Exactly."

Murray was all in hurry-up mode and demanded, "Ladies, can we dispense with the algebraic analogies and get to the point?"

"I make a motion that we recruit another member to Cher's Crewsaders," I announced. Before anyone could interrupt, I spilled. "I hereby nominate Mackenzie Collins to join our team. Who seconds?"

De's jaw dropped. "That is a lame joke, Cher."

"No joke, girlfriend, I *want* her to come aboard."

De was all, "Excuse me, like why would she even want to? Assuming she cared about the Fashion Café, which I think I can say with certainty, she *doesn't,* aren't you forgetting something crucial, Cher? The fact that Mack doesn't even *like* us."

I waved her away. "Tscha, De—Mackenzie doesn't *understand* us. It's like that famous saying, You can't judge a CD by its cover. How could she not like us? She doesn't even know what we stand for."

"What *do* we stand for, Cher?" Summer asked naively.

"Beauty, of course," I replied calmly. "Our posse has always stood for beauty. In this case, beautifying our environment. Mack can't be against that."

Murray started tapping his pebble-soled Hush Puppies and demanded, "I'm not down with this. What do we need her for?"

De and I locked eyes. She suddenly understood what this was all about. We answered Murray's question in one voice.

"Credibility! That's why we need her."

Jesse was predictably flummoxed. "You maxed out your credit cards again, Cher? I'll be glad to take you shopping."

Reason number ninety-six why recruiting Jesse is always a borderline call.

"Not that kind of credibility, Jess. Credibility as in, we need to win this competition. And while *we* know how committed we are to the environment, not everyone sees us in quite that light. We're like brand-name identification. People see us and immediately think, 'campus fashion leaders.' We need them to see us at a different F-stop. We need to be regarded as true crusaders for the environment—at least until we win."

"So Mackenzie Collins will be our mascot?" Jesse asked.

"Unless you know someone else, I think enviro-warrior Mackenzie is, like, eminently qualified for that position."

It didn't surprise me that Murray took an opposing stance.

"Okay, so you all think we need her. What's she need us for? My woman had it right, Mackenzie ain't into that

Fashion Café thing. Besides, I heard she thinks supermodels are the Tasmanian devil. So what's she get out of it?"

During PE, I'd totally thought this through. "We can offer her a forum for self-expression," I explained, "and because of her alignment with us, people might actually pay attention to what she has to say."

I had a killer point, and Murray knew it.

After school I was trolling the Beverly Center, researching ecologically friendly creams, moisturizers, and exfoliants, when I discovered a new brand called Body Ecology. It came in flavors and recyclable tubes. I was deciding between raspberry and papaya body wash when my beeper went off. I buzzed De back immediately.

There was furious honking and other car noises in the background.

"Where are you?" I asked when she clicked on.

"Murray's giving me a driving lesson. We're on Cahuenga, headed toward Sunset."

"You're at the wheel?"

De's inability to concentrate on the road was legendary. That's why she needed extra lessons. "De, maybe right now isn't the best time to be calling me."

"It's okay, you're on speed dial, and besides, Murray punched it in for me," De reassured me. "Anyway, I had this thought, and it couldn't wait. It's this whole thing with Mackenzie. You're not enlisting her because you want to make her over, are you? 'Cause if that's what you were thinking, forget it. A makeover, may I remind you, has to want to be made over. Even subconsciously. And Mack does not give off those vibes at all."

At that second Murray grabbed the cell. "What my woman is sayin' is, memo to Cher: Mackenzie is not a candidate for a makeover."

"As if! Murray, give me back De. Look, I totally wasn't thinking that at all, but now that you bring it up," I said brightly, "I did have one micro thought about how I could improve her life a little."

I was walking over to check out the new Narcisse perfume when I heard it—like, the whole store probably did.

"Swerve to the right, NOW!" Murray was into major decibels, screaming at De. After a few seconds of a jangle of more screams, vicious shouts, and expletives, which I sensed came from another vehicle, De got back on the line.

"Sorry, Cher, that Mazda came out of nowhere. Go on, what were you saying about improving Mackenzie?"

"I mean, I'm not considering her wardrobe—I'm considering her social life. You know my ex-stepbrother, Josh?"

De might not be the sharpest driver, but she does have brutally sharp social instincts. She was all, "Don't go there, Cher. I concede that your matchmaking ability is without peer, but this time you're wandering into totally uncharted waters. Why would a college Baldwin even look at a high school girl, especially if she's not even a Betty?"

De thought Josh was a Baldwin? This was news to me.

"Age is furiously irrelevant here, De, this is romantically correct. Josh, enviro-boy, and Mack, granola-girl. They dress alike, they think alike, they even sound alike. They're practically the same person already. They just don't know it yet."

"With *yet* being the operative word?" De guessed.

"Just concentrate on operating the vehicle at hand, Dionne. Leave the rest to me. With Mack on our side—and Josh at *her* side—it's a total win-win situation. As in, all of us at the Fashion Café on opening night."

Although De and I were miles apart, we did a symbolic limp-wristed high five. I only hoped she left her other hand on the wheel.

Chapter 6

*T*he camcorder had become Amber's most ubiquitous accessory. On Monday, as we congregated by our lockers before first period, she was gripping it tightly. The way you'd hold a gold Amex. Which is what drew my attention to her nails. They were covered in some flaky, dandruff-like substance.

"Your French tips are crumbling, Amber. While they go with your deflating hairstyle, I don't think you did that on purpose, did you?"

Amber gave me a haughty, "I'm not surprised you wouldn't recognize it, Cher. It's Whole Planet nail polish. Environmentally friendly nail polish, that is. It's merely a smidgen of my personal commitment to the Environmental Challenge."

I rolled my eyes. "Earth to Amber, hello—there's a difference between environmental and just plain mental. You're being the latter, not to mention you're littering the hallway with your flakes. Here, have some environmentally friendly nail polish remover," I said, whipping some out of my Prada.

"By the way," I mentioned nonchalantly, "would you also like to borrow my Body Ecology exfoliating creme? Here, smell." I leaned toward her to gloat, I mean, share, my newly discovered line of environmentally friendly scents and moisturizers with her.

Amber turned up her nose at my offers. She was all, "Whatever, Cher. My entire team is racking up personal pledges to the environment. And no matter how much ecological body moisturizer you slather on, you will never catch up with us. So why even bother trying?"

As I scanned the hallway, I could see what she was talking about. Random members of Amber's Angels ambled by. Sean had brought his own mug to school. Amber had obviously talked him into trashing his wasteful juice boxes. Tai was carrying a reusable canvas Keroppi lunch bag.

Okay, so Amber's team might be a few points ahead of us. Whatever. Once I recruited Mackenzie, we would leapfrog ahead of her on credibility alone. So there.

My mission was clear—and immediate. I needed to accidentally on purpose bump into Mackenzie, like, ASAP. En route, I had to figure out exactly how to convince her.

Geist had tipped that Mack was probably in the computer lab. I needed directions, since it's only frequented by the laptop-challenged. Once I found the room, however, finding Mack was easy. Amid a sea of students on their cellulars, listening to Discmans, or flirting with each other, she alone was hunched over the desktop, bare fingers on the keyboard, naked eyes riveted to the monitor. I wondered if being a gung-ho environmentalist meant you had to give the heave-ho to makeup. I shuddered.

Serendipitously, the seat next to her was empty. I slid into it. To minimize distractions, I turned off the ringer on my beeper. Mack, who was wearing sandblasted denim overalls, was furiously engrossed. She didn't notice me.

"Hi, Mackenzie. What's up?" I said innocently but firmly.

I must have startled her, because she jumped. When she turned to me, I noticed that she probably didn't even need a lot of makeup. She had really huge, vibrant eyes. Green, naturally. She peered at me suspiciously.

"Cher Horowitz? What are *you* doing here?"

I'd already decided that, honesty might be like, such a lonely word and all, but it was totally the way to go right here.

"Actually, Mackenzie? I came to find you."

"Why? Did Miss Geist send you or something?" Mack was genuinely curious.

"She didn't send me, exactly. But she did tell me where I could find you. By the way"—I motioned to her computer screen—"you should probably press the Save key. These machines are so Stone Age, you can't be sure they save automatically."

Mack immediately turned to press the Save key, and I glanced at the screen. I caught the words *shall* and *trees*.

"Something for the poetry section in English class?" I guessed. "Like that way famous poem 'I think that I shall never see a poem lovely as a tree'?"

I had to give Mack snaps. She was clearly dying to know why I was here, yet she displayed massive patience. She actually answered my question without asking one of her own.

"No, this isn't for class," she explained. "I'm trying to draft an ordinance to send to the city council."

She tried to measure my degree of real interest. It was majorly solid, I assured her with my rapt expression. She continued, "My friends and I are protesting the haphazard chopping down of trees. You wouldn't believe how many are destroyed, right here in Beverly Hills, like every time some boutique decides it needs a bigger parking lot. So we're trying to get a local ordinance passed that for every tree cut down, there shall be one planted."

Brainstorm! Miss Tree-Saver didn't know it, but she'd just, like, broken off a branch and handed me the ticket to getting her on our team.

Slyly I said, "That's majorly proper. But, well, I don't know how successful you'll be at getting it passed."

"What are you talking about, Cher? What do you even know—or care—about this?" Mack narrowed her green-flecked-with-yellow eyes at me. I was tempted to whip out my lash thickener but held back.

I shrugged my shoulders. "You're right, I don't know that much about, like, tree ordinances. But I do know this. It's like that famous conundrum. If a palm tree gets chopped down on Rodeo Drive, but everyone's at the one-day sale at Saks in the Galleria all the way out on Ventura, does it make a sound?"

Mack's jaw dropped. "Are you all right, Cher?" She clearly thought I'd gone insane. Whoops, my bad. My analogy had totally misfired.

"I guess that was a little obscure. Anyway, what I'm trying to say is, like, okay, you're fighting for tree rights. And that's so profoundly important. But here's the thing. No matter how right you are, or how loud you are, what does it matter if no one hears you?"

"No one has to hear us, Cher, we're writing to the city council."

"Duh, that's my point. Like, why limit it to one fringe group petitioning the city council? Why not get the whole school involved? Make that kind of noise and the city council couldn't possibly ignore you."

"Get the whole school involved. Yeah, right. This school? What planet did you just land from? Most of the kids in this school couldn't care less about trees or any threat to the environment. Most of the kids in this school wouldn't know the difference between fission and fishing! Most of the kids in this school are just like—"

Before she could say "you," I spared her the embarrassment of insulting me to my face.

"Well, I think you're stereotyping us, Mackenzie. But let's just say you're right. Don't you know that famous saying about If you can't beat them, join them? In this school, in case you hadn't noticed, you're totally judged by your peer group. An alignment with us would up your stock considerably. Your message would be heard. See, Mackenzie, I could help you."

Mack was suspicious of my motives. "Why this sudden interest in helping me? And besides, what could you do that we can't?"

"Well, for one thing, my father is an attorney, and I think he knows some people on the city council. I'm sure he could see to it that your bill reaches the right people."

Mack raised her eyebrows. I'd totally snared her interest. And then I sneaked in, "And my ex-stepbrother—don't ask, it's a long story—is like this fledgling law student who's majoring in the environment. He even campaigned to get a pro-environmental

53

state assemblyman elected. At the very least, I bet he could help you with the wording."

Suddenly it was as if Mack could see the clearing in the forest. She snapped her fingers. "I get it. All this time you've been babbling, Cher, I'm all, what is this really about? It's that Environmental Challenge thing, isn't it? Your team is in the running!"

Mackenzie had nailed it, faster and more thoroughly than I would have given her credit for. "You want my help, don't you?"

"I'll be straight with you, Mackenzie. I didn't come for a consult-quickie. I want you to join our team. I want you to be really involved. That's the real reason." As a good-measure afterthought, I tossed in, "Miss Geist is our faculty adviser, and she agrees this is a way righteous idea."

I braced myself for Mack's reaction. Josh, her male counterpart, would have been all, "Forget it. You're just using me. You're not really interested." But Mack didn't say, "Get lost." Okay, so she also didn't say, "Sign me up." She just kind of looked at me, like she was trying to decide. I took that as a good sign.

Then she finally said, "Let me ask you this, Cher. If this Environmental Challenge thing—and its ridiculous connection to the Fashion Café—had never happened, would you even be here? I don't think so." She started to turn back to her screen. But I stopped her.

"You're right, Mackenzie—but only partly. I do care about the environment, and I do lots of things to protect it. I just don't wear my commitment on my sleeve. Just because I believe in fashion and popularity doesn't mean I can't also believe in recycling and clean water and air and all. I'm not one-dimensional, Mackenzie. My friends and I are serious. But you were right about one thing.

We probably wouldn't be recruiting you if it weren't for the Environmental Challenge."

"Well, I admire your honesty, Cher," Mack said carefully, still focusing on her computer. "I'll think about it, okay?"

"Solid. Tell you what—don't commit. Just come to our next meeting and then decide if we're serious enough. It's at my house the day after tomorrow at four. And, Mackenzie? No matter what you decide? I really meant it about helping with the tree ordinance thing."

Mack gave me a tentative grin. Kind of lopsided. Estée Lauder has a shade of lip gloss . . . No, I'm not going there. Yet.

On my way to math I speed-dialed De. She was all, "Cher! I have been beeping you all last period, where have you been?"

If De had a breaking news bulletin, why hadn't she dropped it in homeroom? But I was all, "Wait, me first. I just came from meeting Mackenzie. It's a done deal, girlfriend. She's as good as signed up. I invited her to our next meeting. Only I told her to come early."

"Why'd you do that, Cher?"

"Hello? So she can meet Josh, of course, without all the pressure of everyone being around."

Just as I rounded the corner toward the math classroom, I bumped into De. We put our cells away and continued our conversation.

"What was it you've been beeping me about anyway, De?"

De looked around, as if to make sure the coast was clear or something. "Come with me, I have something to show you," she whispered as we ducked into the girls' room. I knew we'd be late for math, but when a t.b. has something pressing to show you, like, what's the choice? De whipped out a folded-up sheet of computer paper and handed it to me. I fanned my arms to disperse the thick smoke so I could read it.

"Dear Jasmine, I'm ecstatic that we have connected. Although we only just met, I feel like I have known you forever. I feel that I can tell you anything. Fate must have brought us together. Let's meet tomorrow on-line. Same time, same place, okay? Respectfully, Jordan."

"What's this? Who's Jasmine?" I asked.

"Me. I'm Jasmine."

I felt De's head to check for a pitched fever. I'd heard that could make you delusional. But she was as cool as a credit card.

"What are you talking about? When did you become Jasmine? Did you just read *Sybil* for English class or something?"

De giggled nervously. She checked under the stalls to make sure we were alone. "This is so amazing, Cher. Remember when you put me in charge of cyber-research for our fashion show?"

"How could I forget? Did you find anything?"

"Well, I was surfing, trying to get from the Versace Web site—by the way, there was nothing environmental there, though I did find Donatella's family recipe for penne au gratin—to the Armani Exchange. Anyway, I must've misclicked."

"Okay, Dorothy, click your heels and tell me what Oz you landed in."

"Before I realized it, I ended up in Chat Room Three, Row Four. And that's how I met Jordan. Ain't it cute how he signs off 'Respectfully'?" De was morphing into full crush mode. I had to bring her back to reality.

"Dionne! How could you have ended up in a chat room? They're totally populated with randoms!"

"I don't know how it happened, but we got into this conversation, and I don't know . . . it was like our keywords clicked, or something."

"Girlfriend, there are all kinds of psychos on-line, pretending to be people they're not. Don't be naive."

"I'm totally careful, Cher. That's why I didn't give him my real name. I made up Jasmine. Like from *Aladdin*."

Okay, so part of me was relieved that De hadn't gone schizo. But the other part was majorly uncomfortable.

"De, I hate to burst your bubble. But this Jordan character, as intriguing as he may be, is like virtual. Do you not have an actual boyfriend? One with whom you have been involved for several years now?"

"That's just it, Cher. Murray and I have been together so long, we just assume it's supposed to be that way. But what if Murray's not the one? What if my true love is someone else? What if he's out there, and I'm so tied up with Murray that I miss him? Besides, aren't you the one who's always saying I could do better?"

"De, I'm always ranking on Amber, too. It doesn't mean she's not my friend."

"Whatever, Cher. You're not getting it. Do not compare this to Amber. This is big."

This totally wasn't my day for analogies.

Just then the late bell rang.

After math class Murray rushed up to me. The weirdest thing is that I felt a stab of guilt when I saw him! As if I'd, like, accessorized De's cheating or something. But Murray didn't sense my unease. He was all, "Yo Cher, I did that cyber-research thing, and I came up with a whole bunch of enviro-friendly companies. I printed 'em out, but none of them makes clothes. You still think we're gonna pull this off?"

"Leave that to me, Murray," I said sweetly. I actually felt sorry for him just then. He'd done a prodigious job of researching—his list was way long—while all De did was cyber-flirt!

Chapter 7

*D*uring my afternoon classes, I called the companies on Murray's list and ordered up catalogs. I felt sure there'd be stuff I could use for my fashion show.

But I needed that personal commitment thing. Eco-awareness, Josh is fond of reminding me, starts at home. So when I got home, I acted locally, scanning my locale for stuff I could make more eco-friendly.

I started in the kitchen. Thanks to Josh, we already had recycling bins for glass, cans, and newspapers. I subdivided the glass bins into different ones for hues and resin counts.

Then I checked to make sure the dishwasher was totally full. It wasn't, so I crammed more stuff in. Then I hit the energy-saver button and started it. That's when Lucy, who hadn't said a word so far, though I'd totally invaded her turf, protested that none of the dishes would dry properly.

I decided to involve her. So Lucy and I sat down on the floor and judiciously checked the labels on our cleaning products. I wanted to be sure we were using only those marked environmentally friendly. This was way educational for me, as I'd never actually seen a cleaning product up close before. It was fun for Lucy, too, since we scarfed frozen yogurt together as we divided all the stuff into keepers and dumpers. Naturally, we emptied the baddies, rinsed out the bottles, and put them in recycling bins.

"This is so much fun, Luce, we should do this more often," I proposed.

Lucy swallowed the last of the yogurt and nodded.

"What's next on your housekeeping schedule, Lucy?"

She answered by pointing at a basket totally overflowing with clothes. "Wash day," she said, and headed for the laundry room. I bounded up.

"Stop, Lucy! You weren't about to dump all this in the washing machine, were you?"

She gave me a funny look. "They're dirty, Cher. This is how we get them clean."

"Well, we have to rethink our old ways, Luce. Let's call out to the dry cleaner for this stuff."

"There's no need to dry clean these things, Cher. They're all washable."

"That's my point, exactly. Think of all the water trashed to wash them. Our water supplies are way depleted as it is. With *dry* cleaning we won't be wasting water—that's why they call it *dry*. It's way solution-oriented. And majorly chronic!"

Just then I caught a glimpse of Josh, on his way from the den to the fridge. He'd clearly overheard my conversation with Lucy because his eyes were, like, into furious rolling. He was shaking his head from side to side. Seeing Josh made me think of what he'd said earlier about air pollution. Major light bulb!

Josh had jabbered about too many cars on the road, emitting noxious fumes. If I could help cut down on that number, it ought to count for bodacious personal commitment points. Would limo pools not reduce the number of student luxury vehicles on the road and thereby clear the air?

I speed-dialed the limo company Daddy always uses. I calculated we'd need less than a dozen to pick up all the kids in my neighborhood who go to my school—if the limos were stretches, that is. Okay, so it would add some extra charges to Daddy's account, but didn't you get tax deductions from doing good stuff?

Then I started a phone chain, instructing everyone to leave their cars at home. Limos would arrive at their doors starting tomorrow.

I was totally tingling with those do-good killer vibes. So when my phone rang a little later, I practically sang into it, "Zup, girlfriend?"

"Why don't *you* tell *me*, Cher?" sourpuss Amber snarled. But didn't she so have bragging rights to be sour? After all, I was leaping ahead of her on points alone.

Amber was all, "What's this I heard about you forming limo pools to cut down on pollution? Is it true, Cher?"

Coolly I responded, "I can neither confirm nor deny that. You'll just have to show up at school tomorrow to find out, won't you, Ambu-lar?"

"Really, Cher? Well, then, *you'll* just have to show up at school tomorrow to find out about a little something

Amber's Angels have done as part of our *lasting* commitment to the environment. You and your Crewsaders are in for a little surprise."

I could swear I heard her licking her lips when she hung up. But Amber didn't scare me. I only wondered what atrocious shade of lipstick she'd just tasted.

I'd arranged for my limo pool to arrive at school first. I wanted to be there to photograph all the students exiting from their limousines. And to see the expression on Amber's face when she got there.

I couldn't have envisioned a more golden morning. The student parking lots were way underpopulated as limo gridlock jammed the circular driveway in front of our school. Amber was one of the few who didn't agree to the new system. I got a snapshot of her as she emerged from her car, scowling. I was smiling but not too smugly as I explained, "I'm just doing what I can to cut down on those noxious car fumes."

I couldn't cut down on Amber's noxious sneer, however.

De, Murray, Summer, Jesse, and I furiously high-fived each other all the way to homeroom. As we took our seats, I happened to notice that Sean, Jackson, and even Mr. Hall weren't wearing their usual Amber's Angel's T-shirts. Instead, they had new grass green ones bearing the slogan Compost Happens.

Tragically I didn't grasp the full import of that until lunch. As De and I walked toward our table, we noticed a huge contingent—like pretty much the entire student body—huddled in a huge semicircle at the north end of the Quad.

"What's up with that?" De asked, genuinely puzzled.

"Let's do a lap and check it out," I proposed.

We put our trays down and strode over. As we got closer, I could make out . . . Amber . . . and Mr. Hall? They were center stage, in front of a roped-off area. Directly behind them was something resembling a four-foot round mutant soccer ball riddled with random puncture wounds. Next to it was a generic pile of dirt, peat moss, leaves, twigs, and squiggly things.

I turned to De. "Survey says: Amber's formed a soccer team?"

De replied, "And kickoff starts today?"

Not even.

Sean was holding one end of a thick green ribbon that was stretched out in front of them. Tai held the other end taut. Amber was dangerously grasping a pair of sharp scissors and smiling viciously. When she saw me and De, she winked. We shuddered.

Mr. Hall cleared his throat and began, "Welcome, students, to the ribbon-cutting ceremony to dedicate Bronson Alcott High School's brand-new"—with that, he spun around and waved his arm to encompass the mutant globe and pile of dirt behind him—"compost heap. This Bio-Orb Composter was donated by Amber's Angels, to demonstrate our school's deep and lasting commitment to the environment. It is made from one hundred percent recycled polyethylene. Its unique shape will allow us to simply roll it to promote aeration."

With that, he turned to Amber. "Ms. Salk, you may cut the ribbon now."

Which Amber did with a way dramatic flourish that almost took Mr. Hall's eye out. As if on cue—and I am so totally sure they rehearsed this—her cronies began to chant, "Am-*ber!* Am-*ber!*" while heaping furious applause on her. Amber was beaming as she dropped the scissors in favor of her video camera to record the event for posterity. And points.

De and I were major wide-eyed. We hadn't known about this and were severely unthrilled about being blindsided. I surveyed the Quad, which was swarming with students. I questioned how many of them actually knew what a compost heap was—let alone a Bio-Orb Composter. Whatever. They seemed, for the most part, brutally impressed.

Mackenzie and her trail-mix troop were out in full force. If they were perplexed that someone like Amber could get a compost heap happening in the Quad, they didn't show it. I shrugged my shoulders as I waved at Mack. I took it as a good sign that she smiled and waved back.

Just then I saw Miss Geist. I couldn't be sure, but by the expression on her face, I had the distinct feeling that she'd been clueless about this compost heap until now, too. Like, this was her husband's gig, and she was totally not kvelling. What's up with *that*?

Chapter 8

*O*ur limo pools ruled, but I had to face harsh reality. In a battle for points, which would the judges bestow more on? Cutting down on vehicular pollution or cutting up more biodegradable garbage? A borderline call at best. It could go either way.

Our next meeting had to be serious. We couldn't afford to laze around debating where to order in from. Even though I felt way confident that our fashion show would stomp Amber's caught-on-tape catalog of eco-catastrophes, we were woefully behind in those personal pledges. For that, we needed Mackenzie Collins.

On Wednesday afternoon I looked out my bedroom window. The sky was riddled with those cotton-candy, low-flying clouds. Tsuris clouds, Daddy calls them. I checked my Movado. It was almost four, and not a car in sight. I'd just decided to flip on Oprah, when I heard the chimes of our front door ring. I didn't think it was Mackenzie, since I still hadn't heard a car pull up. A split second later I realized, doy, she bikes everywhere. I bounced off the bed, yelling, "I'll get it, Luce!" and skipped down the stairs.

I felt a surge of joy when I opened the door. It was Mack all right, gripping the handlebars of her two-wheeler and looking every inch the granola girl. In fact, in her Z. Cavaricci jeans and Birkenstock sandals, and a T-shirt that read, The Hole in the Ozone Is Directly Related to the Hole in Your Head, she looked every inch . . . a female Josh.

"You don't happen to have a bike rack?" Mack was asking, looking around in what she had to know was in vain.

"Not even," I acknowledged. "Why don't you just park it here inside the foyer? There's plenty of room."

"Am I the first one here?" Mack asked, nudging out the kickstand of her bike.

"Everyone'll show up in a few," I said quickly. "Come, I want you to meet someone first." I led her toward the den, which lately had become Josh-land.

Mack started to follow me, when she stopped suddenly and said, "Who's this?"

I flipped around. Mack was gazing at the portrait of my mom.

"That's my mom. She died when I was a baby," I explained.

Mack nodded. "I can see the resemblance."

Since mom was a total Betty by any standards, I took that as compliment.

"Thanks. But sometimes I wonder if that picture does her total justice. Like, I'm not sure she would have opted for that disco look had she known this would be the last portrait of her ever done."

Mack grinned her lopsided grin. But there was, like,

this trace of sadness shadowing her face. "You're lucky to have this to remember her by. And in a spot where you walk by it every day. It must seem like she's still with you. My father would never allow it."

It took me a while to get what Mack had just said.

"Your mom died, too?" I asked, surprised.

"Five years ago," Mack spoke in a barely audible whisper. "After my father remarried, he got rid of everything that reminded him of her. He sent her clothes to Goodwill, he even trashed her cookbooks and stuff. I mean, my brothers and I have photos, but we have to keep them in our rooms."

"That seems way harsh," I said. "Why would he do that?"

"He won't admit it, but I think it's about Susan . . . his new wife, I mean."

I was processing this startling new info about Mack and, okay, admittedly calculating that having a stepparent gave her even more in common with Josh. His mom was on, like, step four up the remarriage ladder.

"What about your father? He hasn't remarried?" Mack asked.

"He did once. . . ." I started to say, thinking, what a segue into Josh! But before I got very far, we were interrupted by this major commotion coming from the direction of Daddy's study.

"What is this with the paper? Why are we now writing on both sides? How am I supposed to figure out which is current?"

"What's going on?" Mack asked.

"Oh, that's just Daddy. Remember I told you he was a lawyer? He's in his study, arguing. That's what they pay him the big bucks for. Come on, I want you to meet him."

"Are you sure? I mean, maybe this isn't a good time."

"Tscha! Daddy's way into meeting my friends anytime. Follow me."

When Daddy looked up and saw us, he growled, "You have something to tell me, Cher?"

"I have some*one* for you to meet, Daddy. This is—"

"Not now!" he interrupted, impatiently waving Mack away.

"What is this? And where's my shredder?" he demanded, pointing toward a new wall of recycling bins. There was one for mixed paper—white and thermal fax; one for newspapers or downscale magazines with thin, cheesy paper; another for glossy law journals; one for commingled containers like aluminum, glass, and plastic; and one for other stuff like pizza boxes and Chinese food containers.

"They're for paper recycling, Daddy. I ordered them. And I got the agreeable delivery men who brought them to take the shredder away."

Daddy was turning an unflattering shade of red. "And who told you to do this, Cher?"

"Duh, Daddy, no one had to tell me. It's part of my personal commitment to the environment. All that white paper you use should be recycled, not shredded and trashed. I'm acting way locally." With that, I glanced at Mack to see how impressed she was. Mainly, she just looked terrified.

Daddy was screeching toward postal. "And I suppose it was you who told my secretary to use both sides of each piece of paper before recycling it?"

"Aren't you proud of me, Daddy?"

Just then three of Daddy's phone lines jangled in harmony, and his secretary buzzed that Magistrate

Doheny was on the line. As Daddy reached to hit the speakerphone button, he barked, "We'll discuss this later, Cher."

"Is your father always like that?" Mack asked, totally shaking.

"Uh-huh, isn't he adorable?" I led her toward the den.

As anticipated, Josh was there. Only he wasn't reading anything light or unbearable this time. He had a slew of Daddy's depos spread out on the coffee table, and he was downloading some stuff on the laptop.

"Speaking of adorable," I said coyly as I led Mack into the room, "Remember I told you about my stepbrother, Josh? Here he is."

Josh looked up from his work.

"Josh—this is Mackenzie Collins. She goes to my school and might join my team for the Environmental Challenge. She's way into ecology."

Josh looked more puzzled than pleased but stood up to greet us.

"Mack, this is Josh. Even though he's only an undergraduate"—I wanted to be sure she understood that he wasn't that much older than us—"he's way lawyerly already. Especially when it comes to environmental issues. Right, Josh?"

Uncertainty clouded Josh's baby blues, yet he extended his hand to shake Mack's. The sight of them together was awesome. I wished De would get here fast, to bear witness to this historic meeting. Josh and Mack were wearing practically the same thing. Except her T-shirt had that saying on it, while his had a dolphin. They were almost the same height, too, Mack being a good five feet nine. Good thing she's not into platforms.

Since they didn't say anything except mumble, "Nice to meet you," I rushed to fill the awkward silence. "Mack's drafting an ordinance," I declared.

Josh furrowed his brow and said, "Is that so?"

"It's about replenishing our tree supply, right here in Beverly Hills. I told her that since you're an apprentice enviro-lawyer, maybe you could help with the wording."

I expected Josh would have shown a little more enthusiasm. After all, had I not just presented him with a cause *and* a girl that were both completely indigenous to him? But he was all, "I'm kinda busy right now, Cher. Your father is depending on me to finish this."

"Chill, Josh, I didn't mean right now. Mackenzie's got a meeting to go to, anyway. I meant later. Or tomorrow. Whenever."

Mack jumped in. "You know, that's all right, we're probably fine with the wording anyway. Don't worry about it."

Just then the chimes rang, signaling the arrival of my Crewsaders. As Mack and I went to greet them, I felt totally pumped. She and Josh were so awkward! They were already afraid to commit to spending any time together. That's so meaningful!

"Okay, so like this meeting of Cher's Crewsaders will now come to order," I said authoritatively. So what if I did feel like a teacher? We had to get moving and prove our worthiness to Mack. She was sitting cross-legged on the floor of my bedroom, next to Summer. De, who didn't do floors, was on the bed. So was Jesse, who winked at me and said, "This is the first time I've been in your room."

"And the last," I fired back. "We're only meeting here because Josh took over the den."

Jesse just gave me a "yeah, yeah, you don't really

mean that" look. Clueless, that was the word for Jesse. Murray was in the wing chair, casting a loving eye on De. I felt that stab of guilt again, yet plunged into the meeting.

"Okay, so the plans for our fashion show. We're in the preliminary stages. Thanks to *Murray's* thorough work in cyber-research"—I totally eyeballed De when I said that—"we've got a pretty complete list of environmentally friendly companies from which I've ordered catalogs. So that's a beginning—"

"You don't have any clothes for the fashion show yet?" Mack interrupted, sounding surprised. Chronic, she was already getting involved.

"Not exactly, unless you have a suggestion? We'd be profoundly grateful to hear it." All eyes turned to Mack.

"I mean, I don't know how fashionable this is, but there's a lot of stuff out that's made from organically grown cotton. That is, without pesticides or herbicides."

"And on a designer scale, it would be a . . . two?" De said derisively.

"Hello? In this case, the designer is Mother Earth, Dionne," I reminded her gently. Then I turned to Mack. "Proper! Where can I order stuff from?"

"You don't have to order anything, you can just go there. There's a bunch of boutiques along Melrose that carry organic cotton dresses and tops, and stuff made from canvas and plastic—"

"Plastic! Now you're talkin' our talk, girlfriend!" De said, appeased.

"And accessories!" Summer gushed. "I'm there!"

I was utterly amazed that Mack would know that much about shopping. And boutiques. And plastic. Forget about that mascot thing, she was going to be a ferocious asset to our team.

I continued to chair the meeting. "Okay, so next we need to buck up those personal commitment points. Who's doing what?" I looked around the room.

Blank stares all around. "Okay, let's do it this way," I proposed. "We'll list the best topics and then make commitments to them." I thought about Mack's tree thing. "How about trees? Who's going to do something for the trees?"

De raised her hand.

"You don't have to raise your hand, Dionne!" I admonished.

"Sorry, Cher—this just feels a lot like school. Anyway, I sent money to plant a tree in Israel yesterday. On behalf of one of my mother's clients. Does that count?"

"Totally, De, that's righteous. Okay, who's going to commit to water wastage?"

"There is a lot of water wasted right here in Beverly Hills," Mack noted. "People overwater their lawns all the time."

Murray perked up. "Yo, check this. Those lawns are all watered by underground sprinkler systems set on timers. If all the timers in town got, say, slowed down, like, rejiggered somehow . . ."

I rolled my eyes. "I don't think we'll gain points for breaking and entering, Murray." He shrugged his Hilfigered shoulders. "Just tryin' to be helpful is all."

"I've got an idea," Summer ventured. "If we brush our teeth with Evian, there's no danger of letting the faucet water run, and we'll use less."

Mack frowned. "Uh, I don't know, that sounds a little decadent, don't you think, Summer?"

She didn't.

"A better solution might be to limit showers to five minutes," Mack offered.

"Five minutes? As if!" De sputtered. "What about my hair?"

"Hello, ever heard of hairdressers?" I said, way solution-oriented.

"I can think of a way to save water," Jesse murmured. "Shower with a friend. How 'bout it, Cher?"

"As if! Jesse, there's got to be something you can contribute to our team that's not skeevy."

"Okay, I pledge to watch only reruns," Jesse proposed. We all ignored what I hoped was a lame attempt at a joke.

"Jesse?" Mack looked thoughtful. "Doesn't your father run a record company or something?"

"Name the CD you want, babe, and it's yours," Jesse crowed, as if that answered Mack's question.

"It's not the CDs I want, it's the way they're packaged I want *changed*," Mack responded. She explained about how many CDs are rampantly overpackaged with lots more cardboard than is necessary, and about the movement to shrink-wrap them. "Why not look into that as a personal commitment?" she suggested.

I was way impressed. Mack had found something bracingly indigenous to Jesse. I was more determined than ever to lock her into our team.

As it turned out? I will always believe she actually wanted to. When we wrapped, I turned to Mack and acknowledged, "You've been furiously helpful. Does this mean you'll join us?"

Mack surveyed the room. "I don't know if I can be part of the fashion show. I mean, it's not really who I am. But yeah, why not, I'll join. I mean, it's for the most important cause there is. Our planet."

"To the planet, then!" I yelped, and raised my water bottle in a toast. We all clinked recyclable plastic.

"Speaking of the planet," De noted as she gazed out the window, "this portion of it is being rained on prodigiously. We'd better be Audi before the roads flood."

De was right. Those low-flying clouds had suddenly released torrents of water. The upside was that our drought-plagued neighborhood sorely needed it. The downside was that you could get wet.

"Come on, woman. I'll protect you from those cold, hard, driving drops. Take my jacket, so none of that wet stuff lands on you." Murray winked at De, who was all, "Thanks, baby, I'll take you up on that."

I was way alarmed. De and Murray were like, overly compensating with niceness toward each other. They only did that after serious trauma, like a C minus on a math test. But this was just an ordinary day. A day where they should have been sparring.

"Well, I guess I'd better go, too, Cher," Mack said, starting to get up.

"Not even," I said forcefully. "There's no way you can ride a bike through a storm like that. You'll get seriously soaked."

Mack laughed. "This isn't exactly *Twister,* Cher, it's just a few raindrops. No biggie."

"Hello? It will be a biggie if you skid and get hurt," I pointed out. "Why not wait it out here for a while? And then," I tacked on as if an afterthought, "if it doesn't let up, maybe Josh can give you a ride home. I mean, your bike will fit in the back of the Jeep."

Mack looked dubious. But as if on cue, the rain started to pound harder on my skylight.

"Okay, I'll wait it out for a while—I just need to call home, okay?" Since Mack was cellularly challenged, I gave her my remote.

After De, Murray, Jesse, and Summer left, I buzzed down to Lucy for a snack. "I'm massively grateful you agreed to join our team," I said sincerely over hot chocolate and Mrs. Fields cookies.

"I really hadn't made up my mind until I got here," Mack confessed, "but after meeting you . . . and all . . . it seemed, you know, the right thing to do."

Somehow, I got the funny feeling that she'd made up her mind after seeing the portrait of my mom. But I didn't dwell on that thought.

"So, as long as we're waiting out the rain, I might as well pick your brain," I said brightly. "Got any other ideas for my personal commitments?"

Mack surveyed the room. "Well, I don't know how far into this you want to get."

When I assured her of my total commitment, she pointed to my Discman. "Rechargeable batteries make more ecological sense than just tossing out used-up batteries," she noted. I agreed to replace the batteries in all household appliances with rechargeable ones.

Then Mack gazed at my king-size. I thought she was going to compliment the Laura Ashley spread and silk Laurens. Not even.

"There are sheets and spreads that are more ecologically friendly than these."

I immediately grabbed the phone and, repeating after Mack, ordered something called Kalahari textured waffle-weave, from a company called EnviroGentle. But as I finished placing the order, I noticed that Mack seemed a little chagrined.

"I guess you must think I'm kind of over the top with this," she said quietly.

"Not even," I assured her. "When you really believe in something, with your whole heart, you have to be over the top. It's about passion. Something I think I know a lot about."

Mack put her hot chocolate down and peered at me. Very quietly she said, "Sometimes I feel like I'm all alone in my struggles for the earth. Sometimes, I can't sleep at night, because I worry about oil spills and rain forests."

I don't believe, in all my fifteen years, that anyone's ever said exactly that to me. I put my arm around her and swallowed hard. I conjured up my own sleepless nights, which were usually due to some fashion or hair calamity. They seemed somehow less worthy.

But then I looked into Mack's sad green eyes. I realized she was totally reacting to global tragedies with the emotional intensity of an adolescent. She really needs to make the world better.

I thought about my world, full of young people, having fun—something that Mack could use a dose of. There were other things to be emotionally intense about. And focusing on one's personal environment—that is, wardrobe, hair, and makeup—had its value, too. Not to mention the emotional intensity that could be focused on Josh.

"You're not alone anymore, Mack," I said soothingly. "You've got all of Cher's Crewsaders on your side—not to mention all their relatives."

"I'd better get going," Mack said, suddenly a little embarrassed.

"Look, it's still into a major downpour. Let me get Josh to drive you." I didn't give Mack a chance to protest—or Josh an out. I was grinning like that proverbial Cheshire cat when they left together. My mood lasted the entire weekend, which I totally devoted to enviro-research.

Chapter 9

*I*t's Monday, and you know what that means, class. I believe the papers analyzing the quote 'To thine own self be true' are due today," Mr. Hall announced. "I'll be coming around to collect them now." He was still wearing his Compost Happens T-shirt.

When he got to my row, Amber handed him a sheaf of papers.

"This looks like a prodigious job, Miss Salk," Hall said admiringly. Then he turned to me. "Cher, where's your paper?"

"I don't exactly have a paper, Mr. Hall," I began.

"You don't? Well, I'll have to give you a zero, then. I'm very surprised at you, Cher. This isn't like you at all."

"Excuse me, Mr. Hall, I didn't say I didn't do the assignment. I just said I don't have a paper."

I looked around to make sure everyone, especially Amber, was paying attention. "I completely wrote the assignment. And I completely saved paper—and a tree—by E-mailing it to you. It's on your computer. You can mark it and E-mail it back to me. It's a way more ecologically friendly way to hand in assignments."

Hall got majorly flustered. And not in an admiring way, either. He was all, "I'll have to see about that, Cher. I'll just have to . . . see. This is unprecedented."

Instead of giving me props for my brilliant tree-saving effort, he was acting like . . . like . . . he was on Amber's team and didn't want me to get more points. He's her faculty adviser and all, but isn't he supposed to be, like, impartial?

Later, on the way to lunch, I was discussing Hall's rampant lack of impartiality with De, when I totally stopped dead in my tracks. It was the lunchroom. A gleaming new accessory had been added over the weekend: a salad bar. I went to inspect when Amber leaped in front of me.

"Let me be the first to welcome you to Bronson Alcott High's new salad bar, Cher. It was donated by *moi*— with assistance from my team—and features a vast array of organically grown designer greens, including mibuna and mizuma. And I believe"—she pointed to a head of Russian kale—"that shade of green actually goes with that shade of envy you've got on."

Amber smirked and reached into her backpack. "Here, why not start with a granola bar appetizer. With my compliments."

Blindsided again. Like Amber couldn't rest on her compost heap laurels. Or just her compost heap.

I huffed, "No, thanks, Amber. I'll stick with my peach. It's way biodegradable—in fact, it decomposes almost as fast as your hair."

With that, De and I stomped off toward the yogurt

bar. But not before noticing that Mr. Hall was on line at the salad bar instead of his usual, in the teacher lunchroom with Miss Geist.

Okay, it's not as if I was rampantly influenced by Ambu-lettuce, but her salad bar coup had got me thinking. And acting. So the next night, when Daddy called me down to dinner, thundering, "Cher! What is this stuff on my plate?" I was wholly prepared.

In front of Daddy was a veritable rainbow of organically grown and vibrantly colorful cauliflower, zucchini, bok choy, and daikon. It encircled a fetching mound of quinoa, the total new cutting-edge wheat grain protein.

"It's from Yoganics, Daddy," I explained. "They're LA's first organic home delivery service. It's way good for you, and for the environment, too." I looked to Josh, who'd just sat down, for confirmation.

He shrugged his flanneled shoulders and grinned at Daddy. "The new kid on the ecology block strikes again." Then he picked up his fork and stabbed a slice of zucchini. "Cheers, Cher."

Daddy wasn't as immediately accepting as Josh. In the same breath he yelled, "Tell what's her name to call out for pizza!" and "Cher, you've gone too far."

But before I could convince him of the health and ecological benefits of dinner, his cell phone rang and he got into a heated discussion about interrogatories and a pretrial conference.

With Daddy distracted, I sensed opportunity. I totally carpe-ed the diem. "Isn't Mackenzie like passionate about the environment and stuff?" I asked Josh.

"Mackenzie?" For a split sec Josh was confused. Or acting that way.

"Earth to Josh. My new friend, Mackenzie Collins? The one who's writing an ordinance about the trees? The one you, like, drove home? Isn't she a total Betty, in the greenest of senses?"

Josh slurped his Snapple and considered. "She's okay," he finally said noncommittally.

"You two really have a lot in common." I was about to list their raging commonalities when my beeper went off. I would have ignored it in favor of pointing out Mack's many virtues to my clueless stepbrother, but according to the digital readout, it was De.

Good thing I returned the call, too. She was way frantic.

"Cher! I need an interface. ASAP."

Mi casa es su casa, girlfriend. But may I suggest you bike over?" I glanced at Josh so he could see how positively Mack had influenced me.

But De was all, "As if! I'll get there by the usual mode."

"Murray?" I guessed.

"Not. You'll understand when I see you."

When we clicked off, I had the distinctly icky feeling I knew the topic of De's emergency interface. Keyword? Cyber-love. Still, I was pumped that she was coming over. A giant box of stuff had arrived while I was at school, from one of those eco-catalogs. And once De finished spilling all about her virtual crush, we could open it together. Who knows what furious fashion finds might be lurking inside?

De was way out of breath as she bounded into my room a while later. "Did you really bike?" I asked.

She answered me by curling up on the divan, leaning

her head back, and sighing deeply. Then she exhaled and delivered what I'm sure she thought was a bombshell: "He liked *Sense and Sensibility.*"

"He did?"

She nodded gravely.

"Who did?"

De gave me a piercing look. "Who do you think, Cher? Jordan."

Here it was, chapter two in De's cyber-love saga. I wasn't sure how to react. I settled on unfazed and breezily said, "Didn't you also drag Murray to see that?"

"That's the point, Cher. *Drag* is the word. Murray was all, 'What is this sissified girly stuff? Not one thing in the whole movie got blown up!'"

"But this virtual dude, he liked it?" I ventured.

"Loved it. Here, if you don't believe me . . ." De shoved pages of printouts in my face.

"De! All this paper! You know how ecologically unsound this is, not to mention—"

"Just read it, Cher."

I did. It was page after page of mushy confessionals. How stressful it is to be popular. How he feels pressured to adapt this showy urban dialect, to dress flyboy, even if he sometimes wants to wear chinos. How he acts stupid sometimes, and then feels bad about it later. How "I can't talk to my friends about this, but you seem like someone I could really open up to and just be me."

What really surprised me were De's confessions too—how she really liked *ID4!* And how she'd sometimes rather stay home at night, pig out on Chee·tos, and watch videos than keep up her scene-making image. How shopping sometimes seemed . . . pointless?

I was about to call her on that last one, but De was way into infatuation mode. As in high-pitched adulation.

"Cher, don't you see it? He's sensitive, yet strong. He's vulnerable, yet protective. He's"—she gulped—"he could be my perfect boy."

"He's from . . . where?" I asked, hoping it was, like, the Valley.

"Cyberspace. How do I know? All I know is this. Control Shift: Jordan. Keyword: Doable. So what do you think I should do?"

"Do about what, Dionne? First of all, he still thinks you're Jasmine, right? So your anonymity is protected."

"Cher, I want to meet him."

"You've already met him," I quipped.

De narrowed her heavily lashed eyes. "You know what I mean, Cher. Up close and personal. Will you help me?"

"Bad idea, De. What if he's more Billy Corgan than Billy Baldwin? What if it's like this huge disappointment? What if he's . . . certifiable?"

"Well, then, according to you, that makes it a good idea. I'll fly back to Murray, and that'll be the end of it. But at least I'll know I haven't missed my chance at true love. And Murray will never be the wiser."

I considered. De had a point. But she was speeding in the fast lane of the info highway with only a learner's permit.

"De, you're my main big. Would I steer you wrong? My advice is to take it slowly. Trade props with him, but hold up on the interface thing. For a little while longer anyway."

De seemed to be considering, so I added, "Oh, and De? One more thing. Stop printing out this stuff. It's ecologically unsound."

"Cher, you're being unsound . . . like of body and mind." De pouted and folded her arms.

"Whatever, De. Let's file Jordan for a sec and deal with this stuff." I motioned to a huge box in the middle of my room that held our eco-fashion treasures.

"This all you got so far?" she sniffed, unimpressed.

"It's probably a lot of stuff, squished together for ecological reasons."

It took a massive amount of energy, but we finally ripped the gargantuan cardboard open. Instantly a foul odor escaped.

"What's that smell?" De screeched, backing up and holding her nose.

I shrugged. "Maybe it's just been boxed in too long."

I gingerly lifted our first eco-fashion find from its container. I couldn't be sure, but it seemed to think it was a tote bag. As in, it had a strap. It was cylindrical, shiny, black, and rubbery. Hubcaps studded either end. The smell intensified.

"Hello? Like what was it in its former life?" De backed away farther and continued to hold her nose.

"I think it's a tote bag, but it looks and smells like a dead whale," I conceded.

De cried, "This is what they freed Willy for?"

Luckily, it had a label. "Chill, girlfriend. According to the tag, it's a hubcap bag. Made from recycled truck inner tubes. Willy's safe and sound."

"Truck inner tubes? Like from a Range Rover tire?" De asked hopefully. She still hadn't released her nostrils from the pinch.

The hubcaps had a VW logo on them, signifying . . . not. "Negative on the Range Rover connection, De. Okay, so let's toss this in the accessory pile and see what else is here."

"Toss it out on the balcony," De demanded, "or I'm Audi, Cher."

"Don't be such a wimp, De." Still, I opened the sliding doors and did as requested. But not before spritzing the thing—I mean, the hubcap bag—with purifying cologne.

Tragically, I ended up emptying my entire bottle of Narcisse, because all the rest of the stuff in the box had the same smell. Still, I was encouraged by our finds. So was De, who finally unclasped her nose—after I told her it would stay that way if she didn't release it—and helped me model our smelly new eco-treasures.

There were actual mini backpacks. Okay, so they had like a long way to go before making Prada nervous. They were made from those same recycled inner tubes, but accessorized with discarded license plates, which added color and eye-catching detail.

In fact, as we inspected item after eco-item, we got that license plates and car parts were totally the theme. There were purses made from authentic European license plates—more of that Think Globally stuff—and little round bags that were once soda cans. There were road journals with license-plate covers and recycled paper inside, photo holders with plastic inserts, even slim wallets with old bike chains to secure them to a belt loop. Our first boy fashion, which, I was relieved to see, had pockets for credit cards.

"It's like they raided a junkyard to make this stuff— or maybe a prison," De declared as she modeled a backpack with a New Mexico—Land of Enchantment license plate tacked on the back.

"Junkyards are like junior landfills, De. That's what it's all about. Saving the landfills. This is chronic stuff."

At the bottom of the box were a bunch of way

inventive belts. They all featured a seat-belt snap closure and were studded with vintage soda bottle caps.

"I always wondered where the bottle caps went after the bottles got recycled," I said admiringly.

"You never wondered that, Cher."

"Whatever. Anyway, now we know," I said brightly as I clicked one around my waist and checked the mirror. "It doesn't totally suck."

"Yeah, it only reeks," De rejoined.

Soon we had a totally tubular—in the most literal of senses—accessory pile, all out on the balcony. De surveyed it and then slid the door closed.

"Cher, this doesn't seem all that promising. I'm not doubting its authenticity, but how can we pass it off as fashionable?"

"Tscha, De! Remember our goal," I said, visions of opening night paparazzi flashing in my face, "and have faith. This is us, remember?"

Just then the phone rang.

"It's Murray," I said, checking my caller ID.

To him, I said, "I'll put De on."

Murray stopped me. "Hold up, Cher. Better conference it. This ain't no social call. This is a late-breaking bulletin from Sean-Witness News. You both need to hear it."

Since Sean's rep as a big mouth was well-earned, I immediately switched Murray to speakerphone.

"Okay, Murray, we're all ears," I quipped.

"You ain't gonna like it, so do me a props and remember I'm just the messenger here, okay?"

"Murray! Just tell us."

"Okay, here goes." He lowered his voice and went into anchorman mode. "According to a well-placed source—and I am referring to Sean—Amber and her entire team have changed projects. Film at eleven."

"What are you talking about? Changed to what?" De demanded.

"Like I said, ladies, Amber scrapped the video. The whole exposé thing is ex—as in discarded, in the compost heap, probably being devoured by them wormy things. Decomposing as we speak. She's now doin' some presentation on saving the rain forest."

De and I were stunned.

"And in a related story," Murray continued, "Sean and Tai were spotted buying banana costumes."

"How could she do that?" De fumed. "And besides, when did she have time? Is there, like, a rain forest around here?"

I had a vision of Amber in the tropics. And Amber's hair in the tropics. I had to close my eyes. And that's when it hit me. "Not even. I bet she went virtual—like, she accessed a wholly interactive rain forest CD-ROM."

Murray laughed. "Amber in the virtual rain forest? What's that? The bungle in the jungle?" Then Murray got serious. "But I heard it went down another way. Like, Mr. Hall kind of influenced her."

"Why would Hall—" I started, and then remembered that Hall and Geist had visited the tropical rain forest in Belize on their honeymoon. It totally wouldn't be *my* first honeymoon choice, but, whatever. Anyway, they'd brought back like, tons of brochures. Which, I'd be willing to bet my new Cynthia Rowley, were all in Amber's flaky little hands now.

De was still in outrage mode, but my ability to think rationally took over.

"De, check it. If Hall got her to change directions, it

means he didn't have confidence in the winability of her video exposé. We are so totally ahead! The Fashion Café is ours for the taking, girlfriend."

I went to high-five De, but she remained unconvinced. We agreed to totally protest this gross disregard for the rules in school the next day.

Only the way we found Miss Geist in the A.M.? Ixnay on the protest. She was actually sitting down at her desk. And Geist, like, never sat still. Worse, her head was nestled in her arms. I thought she was sick, but as we got closer, I heard the unmistakable sniffling sounds of a woman on the verge.

"Miss Geist? Are you all right?" I asked.

"Can we get you something?" De added, fishing for a tissue in her Coach bag.

Geist accepted it and blew her nose loudly. "I'm sorry, girls. I just . . ." She looked at us. "I guess you heard the news about Amber, right?"

That's why Geist was sobbing? Because Amber switched projects? And people were accusing *me* of taking this competition too seriously? Geist was way overboard. I started to soothe her. "Get a grip, Miss Geist, we can still win."

"No, you don't understand." Geist was all flustered. "I can't, I mean, I shouldn't be discussing this with you girls."

"But, Miss Geist, you can tell us anything. It's us— Cher and De."

Geist let it spill. "It's not Amber. It's not even . . . it's just my own husband, using experiences from our honeymoon so his team can win. I feel so betrayed!"

His team? Geist wasn't the only adult overly identifying with this. I put my arm around her narrow shoulders. I felt the rampant need for shoulder pads. How could Geist and Hall be coming apart? And over this? I was fairly sure neither of them really cared about the Fashion Café.

De whipped out her waterproof mascara as we worked on putting Miss Geist back together again.

Chapter 10

Seeing Geist buggin' like that should have been a sign. The day downsized from tears to jeers. Because of Amber's abrupt U-ie, my team harbored barely concealed hostility toward her. And because Sean had opened his big mouth, her team was all mad at him. Tensions were running high all morning. They came to a head at lunch. It was way *West Side Story*, a verbal rumble between Cher's Chronic Crewsaders and Amber's, like, Turncoat Angels.

Okay, so it might've started when Jesse strolled over to the salad bar, snagged a handful of radicchio, and shouted accusingly, "This is wilted! I wouldn't eat this if it were the last salad on earth. How long has it been sitting here?"

Which gave Sean the idea to redeem himself with his teammates. He was all, I'll defend the lettuce! "I wouldn't *give* you the last salad on earth, man—but it is sitting here all right, thanks to *our* team. I ain't seen nothin' from your side!"

Jesse was cool. "Money talks, dude, nobody walks. I got my father to write a check to the EarthTrust Foundation. I'm saving the earth, not just the rabbit-heads."

"Well, our team donated the compost heap to the Quad." Tai was all, nah-nah-nah-nah-nah. "So there!"

"Big heap!" Summer shouted. "*We* cut down on pollution by forming limo pools! So *double* there!"

"Dudes, I totally shrunk water usage by showering instead of fillin' up the bath! At great personal sacrifice, I might add. So like . . . uh . . . triple there," Jackson bragged. I was surprised at Jackson's arithmetic ability and slightly grossed out now that I knew more than I needed to about his hygienic habits.

Then De strutted over and got in everyone's face. "I got Stoeger and the PE staff to switch to biodegradable golf tees on our driving range! So here, there, and everywhere!" She waved her arms and finished with a flourish.

"Well, I calculated the electrical usage in our entire school and figured out an equation to halve it," Janet Hong, not usually known for confrontational tendencies, sniffed. "So . . . whatever," she added, making the *W* sign. Amber had taught her well. If she'd been on *my* team, I would have taught her something classy.

"Check it, y'all. I got my father to invest big-time in Pax World. Which the ecologically ignorant might not know is a fund that purchases securities in such industries as pollution control," Murray crowed, folding his well-developed triceps across his DKNY Tech chest and winking at De and me.

I was about to say some stuff I did in Daddy's office but was stopped by a voice from behind me. It was . . . Mr. Hall's? "That's very admirable, Murray, but I believe the competition is looking for personal commitments, meaning sacrifices *you* have made. I don't know if your father's investments count."

I was astonished. "Not count!" I began, but got cut off by . . . Geist? She seemed to appear out of nowhere, with her spunk and confidence returned. Not to mention her saved-by-De chronic eyelashes.

"Well, as faculty adviser to Cher's Crewsaders, I, too, have made a personal commitment by riding a bike to school—as opposed to another faculty adviser"—with that, she fiercely eyeballed Hall—"whose contribution seems to be bending the rules by allowing his team to change projects midstream." Geist then sashayed out of the lunchroom.

Her wholly uncharacteristic outburst left all of us—Crewsaders and Angels alike—too speechless to continue our rumble. Mr. Hall just turned toward the salad bar. But not before I saw the tiniest spark of remorse in his eyes.

Though my team had acquitted itself admirably in that impromptu faux debate, I still felt the urgent need for a shopping spree. I was deciding between malls when I realized, "Doy, those boutiques off Melrose that Mackenzie mentioned need, like, prompt attention for our eco-high fashion show." In an impulse move I asked Mack if she wanted to come after school. I was totally pumped when she quickly agreed.

It was way helpful having her, too, as Melrose isn't my normal couture turf. Which might've made power shopping difficult. But Mackenzie led the way toward undiscovered boutiques. We started in one of those retro hippie sandal stores.

"They sell awesome beechwood Dr. Scholl's in here," Mack explained. "They're not only good for your calves, but environmentally sound. And they'll last forever."

Which totally wasn't a plus as far as I was concerned, but then I saw an unmistakable fashion angle. "They come in citrus!" I exclaimed, snagging pairs in lemon, lime, and tangerine. I got my size as well as Mack's.

In another boutique, called Plastic Fantastic, we found a veritable bounty of eco-booty. All sorts of accessories and best of all, a totally dope pair of clingy vinyl hip huggers made from recycled plastic.

I was totally getting into this shopping spree. I actually pulled Mack into the next store. It was riddled with all-natural cosmetics. Okay, so it's not like I was planning to do even a faux makeover on Mackenzie. But fashionally, she was like an unformatted diskette. Would it be so wrong if I programmed her a little?

The next store looked pretty normal to me. "The clothes here are made from all-natural fibers like cotton, silk, and wool," Mack described, "so whatever you think, you know, would work for your fashion show . . ." She trailed off. That was because she saw what I saw—three way familiar people coming into the store.

"Isn't that Ariel, Shawna, and Melissa?" I asked, waving at them.

"Looks like," Mack agreed. Just then they saw us—and promptly did a one cighty and left the store!

"What's up with that? I know they saw us." I was perplexed.

"Well . . ." Mack pursed her lips. "I guess it's because they don't want to hang with us. Or be in the same store as us."

I was stung. "Not even."

But Mack shrugged her slim shoulders and feigned disinterest. She turned and picked up a dress. "What do you think of this, Cher?"

"Mackenzie Collins! Put that down and tell me why they're dissing you! It can't . . . I mean, not because of your membership in Cher's Crewsaders?" The minute I said it, I knew it was true.

Mack took a deep breath. "It's nothing personal, Cher. Not exactly. It's just that they truly believe in a low-impact lifestyle, living in love and harmony with the earth."

"But we believe that, too!" I exclaimed.

"It's just, they feel to really make a difference in this world, we need to move beyond a materialistic mindset. And that careless, self-centered behavior often accompanies unbridled materialistic consumerism."

"And that's what they think of me? That I'm self-centered? And unbridled?"

Mack's silence was my answer.

"Is that what you think, too, Mack?" I said quietly.

"What I think is . . . Okay, Cher, I'll be honest. It's what I used to think."

"But not anymore?" I said hopefully.

"Well, you do shop a lot, Cher."

"Excuse me, but if memory serves, did I not see *them* shopping, too, at BeachSide Mall, and now here? Does that not make them unbridled consumers?"

"They were shopping ecologically. You know, for vintage clothes and recyclables," Mack said defensively.

"I suppose that makes their consumerism bridled, then?"

"Well, yeah, Cher, it kinda does."

"Hello? Like, show me the difference. Shopping is shopping. But we've got to deal with this. They're your friends, and call me materialistic, self-centered, bridled, or unbridled, I do know this. Friendship is more important than any ideology. It's like, what good is a clean planet if you have no friends to share it with? What good is fashion, even? Mack, you need to make them see that an alliance with me will only help the cause—it's our cause now, too."

Mackenzie sighed deeply. "I know, but how I can change their minds? They're pretty adamant. Don't get me wrong, Cher. They're good people. They really care. But it was like, 'Hang with her and you're not one of us anymore.'"

"What made you choose me, then?" I asked, realizing the full import of Mack's massively noncapricious decision. I hoped meeting Josh had something to do with it.

He hadn't. Instead, she was all, "I guess it's what you said about being able to actually get things done. And then when Amber's team got the compost heap, it proved that maybe—don't take this the wrong way—but people like you could get the school to move on these kinds of things. Which would be nice for a change. And also, I don't know . . . I guess I kind of just like you. You're not what I thought you were."

"And you're a lot more than I thought you were," I said, standing on my tiptoes to give Mack a major t.b. hug.

With that, we resumed our hunt and took our eco-fashion finds to the cashier. I whipped out plastic to pay. And that's when I got the total brainstorm of brainstorms.

"Mackenzie!" I shouted gleefully. "What are credit cards made of?"

She gave me that "Cher's gone insane" look. "Uh, plastic, Cher. They're made of plastic."

"Wrong! You forgot to say *recyclable* plastic!"

"So?"

"So this is it—the pièce de résistance of our fashion show. We'll create a wholly recyclable dress made totally from credit cards! This is so dope! We'll even fasten them together with natural fiber string. Or something!"

I wouldn't have pegged Mack for an awards-show buff, but she was all, "It makes sense, Cher, but it's not all that original. I mean, didn't that woman from *Priscilla, Queen of the Jungle* wear one just like it at the Oscars a few years ago?"

"Point well taken, Mack," I acknowledged. Just then the cashier handed me back my Amex. As I slipped it back into my Tignanello wallet, my eye fell on the computer on which she'd totaled our purchases.

Light bulb!

"Okay, so how about a slightly different spin?" I said to Mack. "What if our dress is stylishly riddled with credit cards, but intertwined with something else made of plastic recyclables . . . say, floppies?"

"Floppies what?"

I'd forgotten Mack's lack of computerese. "Floppy diskettes—they're practically Jurassic already, since all the new computers have microdrives only. Floppies have this grievous tendency to self-destruct due to some disease called Fatal Disk Error. Anyway, they're like practically obsolete. If we don't show the world how to recycle them, zillions will end up in our landfills!"

I couldn't tell from the look on Mack's face what she really thought of this chronically brilliant and way ecological idea. She only said, "Okay, but you'll still need a lot of credit cards. Where would you get that many?"

That's when I looked at her as if *she'd* gone insane.

The next few days were like that way famous poem, "Time flies when you're, like, into it." The Environmental Expo was just around the corner, so I put us on a relentless schedule of rehearsals. They were held at my house, mainly so Josh and Mack could bump into each other in a natural setting.

And I'm pumped to report major progress on that meant-to-be front. Josh "managed to find time" in his way busy schedule to help Mack reword that tree ordinance thing. He also promised to get it in front of Daddy, who'd get it in the hands of the right people on the city council.

I couldn't help noticing that Mack wore the citrus Dr. Scholl's on the days she worked with Josh. Would cosmetics not follow?

Everyone was juiced about our fashion finds, especially Summer, who was totally up to the task of stringing the floppies and credit cards together to create a stylish shift. We all had fatal disks to contribute and agreed on gold Amex as the dominant credit card color.

De was our makeup maven. She did wonders with all that natural stuff, plotting colors and contours to go with our fashions. Mack came up with the suggestion that soda cans make excellent hair rollers. Even Miss Geist attended our rehearsals. Tragically, she had lots of time, now that she and Hall were at odds.

We riffed on personal commitments during rehearsals, too. I couldn't get away from the feeling that we needed one more to put us decisively over the top. In the end, it was Mack who thought of it. It would take all of us working together to pull it off, but wouldn't Amber be shocked when I sprang our big announcement during the Environmental Expo!

"Ain't you comin', woman? Miss Dionne, your chariot awaits. And your driver is itchin' to have you snugglin' all close in the front seat." It was way late on the night of our final dress rehearsal, and Murray seemed impatient to leave.

But instead of the "Don't call me woman" rejoinder, De was all, "Hold that thought, lover boy. Gotta do some girl stuff with Cher. Why don't you go snare us some frozen mochaccinos to go at Swenson's? By the time you get back, I'll be ready to leave."

The second Murray left, De sprung it on me. "It's all set. We're meeting."

I didn't have to ask, like, who "we" were. So I just said, "What happened to my advice about taking it slow?"

"Jordan's buggin' about his future," De announced. Like that was an answer.

"And what this would have to do with you is . . . ?"

"Hello, Cher? He needs me."

"Hello, De! What about Murray—he needs you, too."

"Not even. Murray doesn't have a worry in the world—especially when it comes to his future. He's a brilliant entrepreneur. Everyone knows his future is set."

"And this Jordan, what's his future tense?"

"He doesn't know, that's the problem. His family expects all these great things of him. But he's not sure he's down with the stuff they want him to do. Worse, he's not sure if he's really good enough to, you know, live up to their expectations. Oh, Cher, he *needs* me. That's why we've arranged to meet. Thursday night— the beach at sunset."

I let out a long sigh. I wasn't just buying time. De was going to play out this clandestine scene, regardless of what I said. So I did the best I could with what little spin-control I had left. "You're not going alone, Dionne. Don't even try to argue with me," I said decisively. "I'm going with you and that, girlfriend, is final."

"Cher, hold up! I was just going to ask you to come. I may be in love—I think—but I didn't go and get all stupid. I'm allowing for that minute possibility that Jordan isn't who I think he is. Just be a t.b., okay? Trust me, and be there for me."

Chapter 11

What are you doing, Cher? This is bribery!" Josh was in his self-righteous 'tude. And rudely staring over my shoulder as I addressed the gift baskets to the Environmental Expo judges. It was a few days before the expo.

"Excuse me, Josh, this hardly constitutes a felony," I said, bristling. "I'm simply spreading goodwill. And besides, they're Green Being gift baskets, environmentally sensitive with an emphasis on organic products."

I displayed for Josh what was in them. "Each of the male judges gets environmentally friendly shaving cream, and each woman Body Ecology moisturizer and exfoliating creme. Every judge now, thanks to me, subscribes to *E, The Environmental Magazine*. And as a bonus, they can even recycle the baskets, too. It's all part of my personal commitment," I said, affixing a green cause-ribbon to the outside of each basket.

Amazingly, enviro-boy wasn't impressed. "Don't push it, Cher, it's bribery."

"Whatever." I shrugged my shoulders and pinned a green ribbon on Josh's shirt before he could stop me.

Why did it not surprise me that Amber, like, agreed with Josh? When she found out—via Sean, of course—she was all, "That's jury tampering, Cher!"

Our school's Environmental Expo was held in the gym. Okay, it is aesthetically challenged, but it offers the most in the way of spectator seating. Which was way practical, since, like, the whole school wanted to find out who'd win. Besides, all the members of the five teams in competition got to invite their friends, families, and household staffs.

Everything was being videotaped by the tech weenies in the A/V club. The winning tape would then be sent to the Fashion Café to compete with the submissions from the other participating schools.

I totally tingled with excitement as my team set up in our dressing room—the Shannen Doherty Wing of the girls' lockers.

"Did you bring the catwalk?" I asked Summer.

"Check," she replied, pointing to the huge, rolled-up crimson fabric sitting in front of the showers. "I had the fabric store cut it and deliver it this afternoon. It's all set. All Murray and Jesse have to do is ceremoniously unroll it."

Summer had also decorated poster boards plastered with Polaroids detailing our personal commitments. Visuals totally rule over verbiage. There were snapshots of De's tree in Israel, Daddy's wall of recyclable containers, limo gridlock in front of the school, Summer brushing her teeth with Evian, my E-mail with Hall's assignment, Murray's dad's investment slips, and Jesse's dad's canceled checks.

The last poster board was covered up. It held our major, Hall of Fame, out-of-the-park eco-surprise.

I turned to Jesse. "Did you bring the music?"

"One monster soundtrack right here, Cher." Jesse held up our customized mix and winked at me.

"And you know when to cue the A/V staff to start it?" I asked anxiously.

"Gotcha covered. Deejays are set."

All at once we realized that the din from outside the lockers had subsided. We rushed to the door that opened directly onto the gym floor for a better view.

"Crewsaders! Heads up," I stage-whispered. "Judges panel at two o'clock—they're in the first row. Be sure they get the best view of our fashions."

Everyone nodded in grave understanding, even Geist.

I scanned the audience until I spotted Daddy. I was way glad I'd thought to provide him with a cushy pillow and a thermos of cappuccino. Bleachers were so not Daddy's normal seating preference. Next to him was Josh. Lucy, José, and Rico were all there, as were contingents from all the families of my Crewsaders. Even Mack's father and stepmother were in attendance.

The school had given the MC duties to Vice Principal Gardner. At this moment she was standing at that spot on the basketball court where you get the free throws. She redundantly boomed into the microphone.

"Ladies and gentlemen! Welcome to Bronson Alcott High School's first Environmental Expo . . . expo . . . expo!" Her words, like, reverberated around the gym, echoing over and over.

"Tonight's presentations represent the hard work of our school's most dedicated environmentalists . . . alists . . . alists. We know you will learn a lot from each. Our distinguished panel of judges, comprised of volunteers from our administration and faculty, will be tallying points for each presentation. The team with the most points will be announced at the end of the evening . . . ning . . . ning."

Just then someone held up the sign Go Energy-Saving Freshmen! That immediately led to other boosters displaying homemade banners and signs. I couldn't see them all, but I did notice that Dani Loves Danny.

Gardner continued. "The order of the presentations was determined in a random drawing. First up this evening is Scott Berchman and Casey Johnson, who are representing our freshman class. Their topic is, 'Ten Energetic Ways to Save Energy.' Please welcome them . . . em . . . em . . . em!"

Applause filled the gym, and I ducked back into the lockers to supervise the styling of our models. Serendipitously, we'd drawn the last spot on the bill. Our fashion show would be foremost in the minds of the judges. Periodically members of my team, in various stages of undress, dashed back and forth to the door to report on the presentations. When the Energetic Freshmen had finished, De came flying back with a major thumbs-up and the pronouncement "Energetic, but nay for the Fashion Café."

Next up were the seniors. From the little snips I was able to catch, I could see that leaders Courtney and Brianna had done a less than compelling job on that beach erosion thing. Based on the deep tans of everyone on their team, I had the impression they had taken advantage of our unseasonably warm weather and spent more time lying down on the sand than collecting test tube samples and corroborating data.

I raved, "We are one step closer to the Fashion Café."

The third contestant was Igor Azoff and his junior class demonstration on "Pollution—Destiny or Chemistry." While vastly well-intentioned and prodigiously researched, I don't think he gained points by stinking up the gym with canned emissions from car engines, bus fumes, and factory silos. Memo to Igor: Coughing judges are not friendly judges.

In fact, we had to take an unscheduled intermission to get the janitorial staff to open all the windows and defume the place.

An hour later we were ready. My team lined up outside the door this time. We didn't want to miss a single moment of Amber's Angels.

"I bet we catch her cheating," Summer declared.

What we caught, instead, was high drama, Amber style. The gym lights were dimmed. It began to feel sticky and humid as a mist wafted from the corners of the room. Then I heard a sound. "It's the PA system," Jesse whispered loudly. "She's got music, too."

Not even. It was all bird calls and scary bug noises. Way weird. But not to match what came next.

Amber emerged from the boys' locker room. Although she was covered in scratchy barklike material and furious foliage—which seemed to grow directly out of her head like hair extensions—it was unmistakably Amber. As a tree.

A talking tree, that is. When it arrived in the center of the gym, it announced theatrically, "Ladies and gentlemen and members of the jur—I mean, judges panel, welcome to 'The Living Rain Forest' as interpreted by Amber's Angels!"

When the applause quieted, Ambu-tree continued. "Is it hot in here or what?"

To a totally rehearsed audience rejoinder of "How hot is it, Amber?" she gaily replied, "In order to re-create— for your viewing pleasure—the sights, the sounds, and the feel of the rain forest, which is humid and warm, we have raised the temperature in here and set up humidifying fog machines. The sounds you are listening to are those of the birds and insects of the rain forest."

"Not to mention the sound of frizzing hair," Summer moaned.

"How cheesy can you get?" De demanded. The audience didn't agree but rewarded Amber with enthusiastic applause. She launched into her speech.

"Rain forests give us many things, aside from a unique vacation—or honeymoon—experience. Have the canopies of the rain forest not inspired the canopy bed? Have the layers of the rain forest not inspired the layered look? And have the citrus fruits not inspired an au courant fashion trend? Amber's Angels will now demonstrate the breadth and the depth of the many gifts of the rain forest."

At that moment a six-foot-tall walking banana emerged from the boys' locker room. It was yellow and smooth skinned, and would have been way convincing had it not strutted like a flyboy. "It's Sean, in a banana costume," Murray announced unnecessarily. "Bring on da potassium!"

It spoke. "I am a banana," it said. "I represent the food of the rain forest. My brothers and myself— pineapples, Brazil nuts, and citrus fruits—give us healthy food to feed our planet. And we get props for coffee, too. Where would all them designer coffee bars be without the rain forest, I ask you!"

The banana was getting way impassioned. He flashed a peace sign and ended with, "Big up to my peeps!"

Tai was next. She was festooned with brightly colored poster board cut in elongated triangles. They started at her neck, tucked into her collar and pointed outward. I couldn't decide what she was. "Court jester?" I guessed.

De rolled her eyes. "Hello? Total pineapple."

Not even.

"I am a bromeliad," Tai announced. "I represent the plants and animals of the rain forest. One quarter of all prescription medicines have ingredients that come from me. Well," she said shyly, batting her eyelashes, "not me personally, but all my rain-forest-plant homies. That includes antibiotics and tranquilizers. Where would we be without *them*?" The audience let out a collective gasp.

Janet followed Tai. She was covered from shoulders to Sam & Libby's in a drab muslin potato sack, spray-painted in gray. She carried an open umbrella in the same unflattering shade. "An elephant trying to keep dry?" Summer guessed.

But in a clear voice Janet rang out, "I am fungi."

I don't believe that statement had ever elicited such an animated response from any audience anywhere. Janet continued. "I live on the floor of the rain forest and help recycle leaves that have fallen from the canopy above. They release their goodness for trees to take up in their roots."

Amber's team was gathering steam. On the heels of the fungi was Jackson Doyle. They'd painted his face in deep stripes of primary colors and awarded him with a feathered headdress and toy spear. I totally would have rethought that last prop.

"Yo, I am an indigenous person. I represent all two hundred million indigenous people. My posse is farmers and hunter-gatherers like me." Jackson launched into short, declarative sentence fragments. "I hunt! For food! I fish! In clean rivers! I eat! Fruit! From the trees! I cure illnesses! With medicines from plants!"

"I've never seen him so animated," I whispered to De.

"It'll take him all next semester to catch up on his sleep," De commented.

Jackson's flashy finale was "My posse and me have learned to live in peaceful harmony with a fragile environment. We have not destroyed the forests or polluted the air. We could help you learn"—with that, he thrust his spear at Principal Lehman, in the first row, who ducked reflexively—"but I am being *obliterated*, man! By *you*, man!"

I'd like to report that Jackson didn't chuck his spear just then, but I can't.

"If he hits the principal, more points for us!" Murray gloated.

And then it was Amber's turn. She stepped onto center stage and announced, "And I, Amber Salk, am a banyan tree." Then she bent over so that her hands touched the floor and her butt was in the air.

"Miss Thing needs to prove she's in shape?" De huffed.

"Duh. She's pantomiming the downward growing roots of a banyan tree," I explained. "Crude but accurate." Amber actually did her speech upside down.

"I, Amber Salk, represent all the trees of the rain forest. *I* provide paper, fruit, nuts, lumber, and places for birds and animals to live. *I* affect weather, worldwide.

I reduce floods, *I* give the world oxygen and clean air. My leaves are like solar panels that soak up carbon dioxide. I filter dust and soot from the wind. *I* am irreplaceable."

"Well, she got that right," De deadpanned.

Amber gathered her team around her as she straightened up.

In unison they announced, "Together, we are an ecosystem, a place where all living animals and plants coexist. We get our energy from the sun and are proudly codependent on our environment. Together, we give of ourselves unselfishly."

Then Amber took one step forward and lapsed into faux indignant. "Excuse me, my fellow Americans, the rain forests give and *give* and *give* unselfishly of themselves, and what do they get in return?"

Silence. Amber whirled around and repeated louder, "I *said*, what do they get in return?"

Mr. Hall emerged from the boys' locker room. Because he was dressed in a suit and tie, I wasn't sure what vegetable, animal, or mineral he was supposed to be. I thought maybe a take-out meal because he was carrying a fistful of chopsticks.

Hall cleared his throat. "I represent corporate greed and the plundering of our unsullied wilderness. Yes, I am a logger. Me and my . . . posse?"—he glanced uncertainly at Amber—"are pillaging the resources of the rain forests for our own greedy purposes. We exploit them for the almighty buck. We chop down trees and make chopsticks. We slash and burn the rain forest to raise cattle for cheap hamburger meat. We are the enemy of the rain forest."

Amber had worked herself into a faux rage. "Yes!" she screeched. "Because of corporate greed and government boondoggle, the loggers are winning! We must beat them back! We must harness our resources! We must say NO to chopsticks!"

With that, she grabbed them from Hall and flung several pairs in the air. Everyone ducked. It was a drive-by chopstick attack.

"We must say NO to fast-food hamburgers made from rain forest cattle! We must say NO to rosewood, mahogany, teak, and ebony! We must say YES to rescuing the rain forest!"

Jarringly Amber switched cadences from high drama to the low road. "And as a reminder of the importance of our tropical rain forests, each member of the audience will go home tonight with a reusable tin of Rain Forest Crunch Candy, as a lovely parting gift."

Then Amber the banyan tree took a deep bow, as did Sean the banana, Tai the bromeliad, Jackson the indigenous person, Janet the fungi, and Hall the logger.

The applause was deafening. The cheers "Amber's Angels rule! The rain forest rules!" pierced the fog-machine-induced mist. And then I totally could not believe my eyes, the entire gym erupted in the wave! It started at Amber's parents' section and went all the way around the bleachers. Except for lone holdouts Daddy and Josh, it was all encompassing.

Amber totally staged this—and she accused *me* of jury tampering?

The specter of following Amber now seemed like lowly Liz Claiborne following, like, Versace at the Paris shows. Still, I didn't want to undermine my team's spirit. I took a deep, calming breath and called everyone around for like, a pregame huddle. I didn't know what to say, so I went for the way rallying "Let's go teach them something about fashion—and ecology!"

The time was now, but just as Vice Principal Gardner

started to introduce us, a monitor burst through the door into the girls' lockers, shouting, "Telegram for Cher Horowitz! Telegram for Cher Horowitz!"

I didn't know you could send telegrams on napkins. I unfolded it and read it out loud.

"I may not always agree with everything you do, but I'm always proud of you—never prouder than tonight. Break a leg, Cher & team. Love, Daddy. P.S. Mom says, 'You go, girl!' "

I held it to my heart and then stuffed it into my dress. And that was all it took. My confidence was fully restored. As I signaled Jesse to cue the deejays, and strutted out, I felt rampantly secure. Let Amber have her rain forest moment. Cher's Crewsaders were about to give her a Michael Johnsonian run for her money. And immortality in the Fashion Café.

In my clingy, floor-length, and way ecologically viable Alaïa shantung shift, I was totally the bomb. I saw Daddy, Josh, and our aides-de-camp clapping wildly and giving me double-digit thumbs-ups. Jesse and Murray ceremoniously unrolled our catwalk, and Summer placed our personal commitment poster boards in front of the judges.

I smiled broadly and made sure I fully involved everyone as I declared, "Honored guests, welcome to 'Eco-High Fashion: Original, Indigenous, and Way Cutting Edge' by Cher's Crewsaders. Like our worthy predecessors"—I generously acknowledged Amber, who was against the back gym wall and hanging on to my every word—"we, too, believe in the rain forest. We, too, are committed to a clean planet. But *we* cannot tell a lie. We must be true to our own selves—and as indigenous people of Beverly Hills, we are also committed to high fashion. Oxymoronic, you say? Nay, we say! We believe fashion is life. We believe in that life on a clean planet." The audience was totally with me.

"We must live in harmony with the earth. The good news is that we can do that and still be fashionable. Tonight we will be to our own selves, true, and to our planet, truly responsible. You are about to witness the first Eco-High Fashion Show ever on any planet. The way inventive fashions and accessories in this unique collection are made from recycled materials that otherwise would end up in America's junkyards, landfills, and incinerators. So sit back, enjoy, and learn as Cher's Crewsaders stylishly link personal and planetary ecology."

I motioned to Jesse to signal the music and drew everyone's attention to stage left.

"Our first model tonight is Summer." On cue, Summer came out and headed straight down the catwalk. She was swaying to the beat of Juliana Hatfield's "I Wanna Be a Supermodel" off our monster soundtrack.

"Summer is wearing the latest in eco-high fashion. Her hiphuggers are made of wholly recyclable vinyl. Her crop-top T-shirt is organic cotton, her ankle-strap platforms are plastic jellies. Summer's looking good—while doing good!"

The appreciation for Summer was way palatable as she did the catwalk, twirled, and hung by the judges an extra few seconds before heading backstage.

My narration continued. "Okay, so like have you ever wondered, as I have, what becomes of the bottle caps when we recycle our bottles? Wonder no more, for here comes Jesse," I announced, "who's about to answer that question. The seat-belt-closure belt snugly around

Jesse's waist is riddled with vintage bottle caps. It's stylish and ecologically sound. Note, too, that Jesse's wallet is attached to his jeans loop by recycled bike chains. Jesse's in no danger of losing his credit cards!"

In a move he'd totally practiced, Jesse thrust his waist—and his butt—around grandiosely as he strutted like a peacock to the beat of the Dr Pepper commercial. Jesse was massively appreciated by the ten-year-old girls in the audience, who shrieked nonstop.

I went on. "Thank you, Jesse. Now, what about eco-fashion in the privacy of your home? Our very own Miss Geist is here tonight to demonstrate just that." To the tune of "Manic Monday," Geist, her hair totally wrapped in rollers made from steel food and beverage cans, smiled gamely as she headed down our catwalk. She brandished a bicycle handlebar hairbrush, which had been recycled from an old two-wheeler—way authentic, with the tacky streamers still in place. Geist gained confidence with each step as she strutted in her cotton knit chemise and kimono. She was totally kvelling from ear to ear. I sneaked a glance at Hall, whose face told it all. He was rampantly in love with her!

"Thank you, Miss Geist," I said, nodding appreciatively in her direction. "Our next model is Mackenzie, looking furiously fetching in an organic cotton crop-top T-shirt made from recycled pop-bottle fleece. Mackenzie's fashionable footwear is Dr. Scholl's citrus sandals. And tonight Mackenzie has accessorized her look with a hubcap bag."

As I described the ingredients of Mack's bag and top, I peeked at Josh, who was clapping wildly. It had taken serious negotiating to get Mack to agree to model, but by the look on Josh's face, it was all worth it. The tune

Jesse had chosen for Mack, "Closer to Free," was on the money, too.

"Excellent, Mackenzie! Thank you." She was beaming as I continued. "Okay, so next. It's like that famous saying, Accessorize or die! Here comes Dionne, doing accessories the recyclable way."

De shimmied down the catwalk, fully accessorized in that formerly smelly rubber backpack, fully recyclable cell phone at her ear. As she passed the judges, she twirled and leaned her back into them, so they could fully appreciate how fashionable a truck inner tire could become. I waited until De had sashayed back to the lockers before my next announcement.

"Next, we have something special for the girls. Give it up for Murray . . ." I started, but just then the shriek barrier exploded. It had been total inspiration to do Murray shirtless, in recycled cotton Calvin-clone boxers. With his defined cuts, sweaty because the gym was still permeated from Amber's mist machine, Murray was way Tyson Beckford. Could De not have noticed?

I had to shout to be heard above the kiddie screams. "Okay, so I know most of you aren't focusing on his head, but if I can draw your attention there, note the cap that Murray's sporting. Not just any baseball cap, it's an Eco-head cap, made entirely from hemp."

I had planned for Murray to be out longer than anyone else, not just to give the women judges ample ogle-time (though I told him not to bother vogueing for Stoeger) but to give De enough time to dress for the next ensemble.

When the applause for Murray had finally quieted, I announced, "Every collection must encompass something hugely unique, and so does ours. Ladies and gentlemen, I now direct your attention stage right, as Dionne's about to show you that CDs, constructed of recyclable plastic, are not merely for listening anymore."

If I was the bomb, De fully detonated the place. She was swathed from sculpted shoulders to shapely legs in the only-one-of-its-kind dress made entirely from CDs! Held together by circular plastic rings, the CDs were draped over a translucent sheath and strategically situated all over De. The dress had been my light bulb, Jesse's inspiration, and Summer's execution. Teamwork at its most chronic.

De's catwalk music was "The Electric Slide." And although she swore she wouldn't, she totally got caught up in the moment and danced her way down the catwalk. The entire audience caught the spirit, bouncing up from their seats and following De's electric slide steps. Later Daddy told me he thought it was the hokey-pokey.

When De came around to me, in a rehearsed move, I quickly passed the microphone to her, and ducked into the girls' locker room. There Geist, Summer, and Mack helped me slip out of the Alaïa and into my pièce de résistance, the gold Amex credit card and floppy sheath.

I felt a rush of adrenaline and excitement as I heard De announce, "And now, our final model of the evening, wearing our most indigenous piece—please welcome Cher, in her credit card diskette dress!"

The welcome from the audience was warm—as in scalding. The spotlight was mine, and I totally danced, pranced, and pirouetted in it. I felt like I was walking on smog-free air. My music was "The Shoop Shoop Song." When the cheers of "Go, Cher! Go, Cher!" had subsided, I retrieved the microphone from De.

"Thank you, everyone, for your enthusiasm. We urge you—keep on shopping! But buy recycled. Keep on shopping. But shop green retailers, too. And remember, less packaging doesn't mean skimpier clothes. It means, take your skimpy clothes home in less packaging. Share shopping bags! And shop for a better world! But above all, shop!"

When the applause subsided, it was time to reveal our surprise. I stepped forward.

"Cher's Crewsaders have fully demonstrated the link between fashion and ecology. But that is not all we have done. In researching our project, we became totally inspired. It's like that way famous poem, 'We believe we are never so tall as when we stoop down to look in a bargain bin for a great deal on a designer shirt.' So it's like the same thing here. We're never so tall as when we stoop down to, like, help the earth.

"Therefore, I now proudly unveil Cher's Crewsaders' majorly chronic team spirit commitment. As a brilliant, idealistic man once told me"—with that, I looked up at Daddy—"if you're not part of the solution, you're part of the problem. Tonight Cher's Crewsaders are way solution-centric. Jesse—the music, please."

The PA system squawked.

"What you're hearing is a track from *MOM: Music for Our Mother Ocean* by Chris Isaak, Eddie Vedder, and Perry Farrell. And what you're about to see totally complements the music."

I turned to Mack and De. "Girlfriends, unfurl our final commitment board."

And there it stood. A huge photograph of the ocean, riddled with a fleet of cruise ships.

I read, "All life on earth depends on water. But are our

rivers, lakes, and oceans not being poisoned by pollution, garbage, and nasty chemicals dumped into them? Cher's Crewsaders, with backing from the firm of Mel Horowitz, your friendly Lexus dealers all over town, the alliance of Los Angeles record companies and movie publicists, plus substantial support from the parents of Summer and Murray, have banded together to purify our ocean.

"We have contacted the Rendezvous Cruise Lines—a major polluter—and demanded the cleanup of the toxic sludge they routinely dump into our ocean. With our support, we will help them find another means of waste disposal. If they refuse to comply, they risk being boycotted by every member of the chamber of commerce of Beverly Hills, with which we hold major influence. We will no longer allow our oceans to be polluted by luxury cruise ships."

It started with a collective awe-inspired gasp from the audience. Then the gym erupted in wild applause, standing ovations, whistling, jumping up and down, and lots of arm-pumping "Whoo! Whoo! Whooing!"

I looked up at Daddy, who was leading the cheers. Out of the corner of my eye, I saw Josh. He was just about to toss a bouquet of flowers, so I ducked. Mack caught it. It was so cute the way she and Josh wore the same surprised expression.

We were still basking in the limelight when I heard Murray yell, "Cher! Heads up! The judges are back." I hadn't realized they'd been gone, but here they were, all in their seats, handing an actual envelope to Vice Principal Gardner.

"If everyone could please quiet down, the judges have tallied up all the points earned by our teams," Gardner announced, stepping up to the microphone. "The winning one is in here. But before I open it . . ."

De rolled her eyes, "Why do they always do that stalling tactic?"

Gardner droned on, "I know I speak for the entire student body, faculty, and administration of Bronson Alcott High School, as well as everyone in this room, when I say, regardless of what is in the envelope, you are all winners. You have all demonstrated commitment to our planet, and we have all learned something tonight. We are proud of all of you."

We may be all winners, but, hello? We're not all going to the Fashion Café.

"And now, without further ado, the winner is . . ." My team formed an impromptu circle. We held one another's hands and closed our eyes. Then we heard Gardner gasp, "Oh, my—it's a tie."

I totally couldn't believe I heard someone say, "A Nicole Miller?"

Then Gardner announced, "Our first winner is . . . Amber Salk! That is, Amber's Angels for their rain forest exhibition."

Amber's team totally took up excess time whooping and jumping and hugging and high-fiving.

Then Gardner continued. "Our other winner is . . ."

I sucked in my breath. My stomach was totally having a Kerri Strug moment.

"Cher's Crewsaders! And . . ."

I didn't hear the rest. Our cheering, whooping, jumping, hugging, and high-fiving was hyper-energetic—louder, longer, and more frenzied than Amber's any day.

All at once the bleachers emptied onto the floor of the

gym, and we were rushed by a mosh pit of well-wishers. Our whole family of friends all came together in planetary alignment to encircle us with love and affection. I threw my arms around Daddy's neck. Over his shoulder I saw Mack, doing a three-way hug with her father and stepmom.

Chapter 12

Okay, so I would have preferred the win to ourselves. But it's like, if my ensembles have to squish together in one shopping bag for the good of the earth, I guess I can make room for Amber in my Fashion Café exhibit. Besides, I didn't really have a choice. As the judges had decreed, Amber's Angels and Cher's Crewsaders had to, like, Brady Bunch it—that is, blend—to create the permanent display to represent our school at the Fashion Café.

Naturally, after all the schools in our district sent their submissions, ours won. You had to give the audiovisual nimrods snaps for how they'd edited our presentations together into a totally seamless presentation. There was even talk about it being submitted to Sundance.

But in all due modesty, I can't really say this was like a surprise. Of course we won. Like whose would they choose over ours? Murray and Sean, the gruesome twosome together again, had accessed the submissions of the other schools. Talk about lame! Talk about pathetic! One from Pacific Palisades High was a video exposé. And, like, where had I heard that one before?

Another upside was that Hall and Geist would now be thrown together—something I sensed they were way ready for. But they needed a push. They were still totally masking their real feelings for each other. It was during one of our creative meetings to design our exhibit that I got my chance to make that happen.

After protracted negotiations, we'd settled on what our exhibit would be. We decided to dress a Madame Alexander doll in a replica of my credit card-diskette sheath. At her sandaled feet we'd prop up mini representations of all our inner-tire accessories. Amber's team's contribution was that our eco-high fashion doll would be standing in a re-creation of the rain forest. Summer, in charge of set decoration, had even accessed a book called *Make Your Own Rain Forest,* which included a giant, three-dimensional press-out rain forest model.

"The tree should be bigger!" Amber whined. Summer was way exasperated and gave me a pleading look.

"Hello? It's all got to fit in a three-foot-high glass display case, mounted on the wall, Ambu-lamebrain," I reminded her. "Your tree can't be any bigger or the fashion aspect will be minimized."

"And it is called the *Fashion* Café, is it not?" De reminded her.

I turned to Hall. "Don't you agree, Mr. Hall, that the rain forest element, which will be encircling our entire doll, is best blended into the scenery rather than upstaging it?" Then I added slyly, "Miss Geist always says you have the most rampant eye for detail of any man she's ever met and—"

"She does?" Mr. Hall got all flustered and looked over at his wife.

"And I know you're always saying how poetic Miss Geist is when she's passionate about something."

Geist blushed.

"And I know I speak for our totally blended teams when I say we will all abide by whatever decision the two of you come to. You are both our faculty advisers, after all."

Amber was all, "Excuse me, we have an exhibit to finish!"

De shushed her and said to Hall, "Why don't you and Miss Geist take a cappuccino break and discuss it? We can pick up where we left off tomorrow."

Miss Geist, who hadn't said anything up to that point, totally batted her chronic eyelashes—I'd given her the mascara to keep—at Mr. Hall. "I guess that would be okay with me," she finally sputtered.

Mr. Hall flashed a dazzling dental display as he extended his arm to help Miss Geist up from her seat. "Shall we?"

I felt a complete sense of wholeness as I watched them walk out together. Well, one third whole, anyway. I still had two to go.

I was totally giving myself snaps for implementing Hall and Geist's reunion as I sat down to dinner that night. Daddy was on the phone with the Rendezvous Cruise Lines, threatening the major boycott we'd promised. I gave him a peck on the cheek.

"You've been so massively supportive, Daddy," I said

as he pressed End. "I know this ecology thing isn't your like, bailiwick."

"I haven't completely changed my mind, Cher," Daddy said. "I still think some people take it too far. But I also think we've all learned a lot in the past few weeks, thanks to you and your school friends. The environment is all our bailiwicks. And on that note, I have a little present for you."

Daddy reached into his wallet and whipped out . . .

"A new credit card! Oh, thank you, thank you, thank you, Daddy!" I jumped up and hugged him.

"It's not just any credit card. Look at it, Cher. I believe this is a credit card that's . . . let's see, how would you put it? Way indigenous to you?"

I laughed. Daddy was so cute when he tried to imitate me. But he was right about the card. It came with a note. "Congratulations on your new Working Assets credit card. Every time you use it, a percentage of your purchase goes to nonprofit groups like Greenpeace . . . at no extra cost to you. You turn your everyday purchases into acts of generosity. It's plastic with a purpose."

I was way moved. "Daddy, this is so massively . . . indigenous! And since I'm totally helping the environment every time I use it, I guess my credit limit must be way high."

"Don't push it, Cher," Daddy said, all faux-gruff.

"I love you, Daddy."

"I know, Cher. I love you, too."

Like that way famous saying "Love is in the air," that's totally how it seemed in the days following our fashion-show coup. Of course, love sometimes couldn't find its way out of paper bag—which is why it needed me. And which is why, in a strange way, I was pumped that this way ridiculous Jasmine-Jordan thing was imminent. De would not be talked out of it. So I figured, one look at this Burbank Barney, and she'd totally go flying back to Murray.

"Ready, De?" I'd buzzed her just before leaving the house to pick her up.

"I think so." De was all breathless, even though she hadn't gone anywhere yet. "I can't decide what to wear."

"Personally, De? I've never met a cyberdude, but if it was me? The entire event totally screams 'backless Calvin.' Elegant, simple—and a fully 'I am not trying too hard' design statement."

"You think?" She was all nervous.

"Stop biting your nails," I cautioned. Even though I couldn't see her, I knew her left thumb was trashed by now.

"Okay, okay, I'll do the Calvin. Give me ten extra minutes."

"Fix your acrylics," I reminded her.

In the cab on the way to the beach, De was all, "I keep picturing what he'll look like. I bet he's way Denzel . . ."

" . . . or Will Smith, with those Dumbo ears." I giggled. Which De totally did not appreciate, so I amended, "Okay, he might be mad cute. He might have that George Clooney thing happening with the hair. . . ." De brightened. But I couldn't stop myself. "Or he might have the Kramer thing happening with the hair!"

I totally burst out laughing, for which De elbowed me sharply in the ribs.

The sun was just grazing the horizon when the cab dropped us at the beach in Santa Monica. "Isn't this where they tape *Baywatch?"* I asked De, partly to get her mind off the upcoming moment of truth.

"Baywatch? Who cares? What do you think he'll think of me, Cher? What if I disappoint him?"

"Tscha, De! Disappoint him? You are fully chronic. Like, move over Naomi!" I wasn't exaggerating. De had taken my advice and done the backless number. I only wished she'd consulted me about the footwear. There's something about five-inch-high Manolo Blahniks and the beach that does not compute.

I never really understood the romantic appeal of the beach before. Sand totally gets into your designer sandals. The ocean-bearing breezes spell disaster for your hair. And whoever thought being surrounded by randoms, like, promoted romance? But tonight it seemed different somehow. Maybe because it was one of those sherbety pink starry evenings with a mere low-grade smog alert. Even the breeze, like, blew my hair in the right direction for a change.

"This feels so magical," De whispered as if she'd read my mind. "Murray would never think of it."

Murray. She's still thinking about him. Excellent. As I scanned the sand, I asked, "So like, did this virtual Jordan dude say how you'll recognize him? After all, he won't be bringing his computer screen—or, hello, his printouts—to the beach, right?"

"Cut the sarcasm, Cher. Jordan is real. Which you will find out soon enough. I may not know exactly what he looks like, but I will know him when I see him."

"How, De?"

She rolled her eyes. "Not that it's necessary, but he said he'd be carrying a copy of *Sense and Sensibility,* okay? Is that good enough for you?"

"And he reads, too. Impressive," I deadpanned, still looking around. "And what about you—any identifying birthmarks or scars you told him about?"

"Jordan says he'll know me when he sees me. He'll recognize me by my aura."

"Really? So he's been in touch with his psychic friends?"

"Tell me why you're here again, Cher? If you're not going to be supportive, why not just be Audi?" De was starting to bug big time.

"Sorry, De. I'll ride the shame spiral for that one. But, seriously, what did you tell him?"

"Just that, uh, in case, you know, someone else had a similar aura that I'd be the one wearing the double-strand necklace with the pearlized baby hearts," she answered, pointing to the accessory that, as I recall, Murray gave her. To my t.b. credit, I left that observation unsaid.

I continued to scan our locale, but no book-wielding Baldwin—or Barney, for that matter—materialized. "Okay, so did Jordan say like, exactly where on the beach to meet? Maybe we're in the wrong spot."

De's spiked heels sank deeper and deeper into the sand with each step we took.

"Near here, I think," she said, looking furtively around. "I'm sure he'll show up at any minute. Let's just keep looking."

But all I saw, looking around, were clumps of generics. The beach was totally dotted with them. Singletons listened to music; couples cocooned. I did notice where the beach was completely eroding and how the trash patrol, like, needed to get its rear in gear. Out in the ocean the surfer dudes were riding their last waves of the day. As I swung around to eyeball the street leading to the beach, suddenly I saw something way familiar, in a vehicular sense.

"Look at that Beemer parked over there"—I motioned to De—"Doesn't it look just like—"

Before I could finish, a rampantly studly form alighted from the car. He was too far away for me to detect the logo on his tank top—but if I had to make a call, I'd go for Hugo Boss. Over one arm, he seemed to be carrying a blanket. In his other hand, he grasped a profusion of gaily colored flowers.

He was still pretty far away, so at first glance, I couldn't make out his features. But a half-second later I realized I didn't have to. It was the walk. A walk I'd totally recognize anywhere, especially as it advanced toward us. De saw it, too.

"Ohmygosh, what's he doing here? You told him, Cher! How could you? You betrayed me!" De shriek-whispered, halfway into a hissy fit.

"Dionne! Get ahold of yourself. I would never do that. And you so know it."

"Then what's he doing here? And where's Jordan, anyway? Oh, Cher, you think he stood me up?"

As the studmuffin advanced toward us, recognition, and what I'd totally classify as fear born of guilt crossed his braces-face.

De dived right into screech decibels. "Murray! What are you doing here? And what's up with those flowers? You hate flowers!"

Murray zoomed into the offense zone. "What—what am I doing here? I could ask you the same question. You and Cher hate the beach. Ain't you always sayin', 'Sand gets in my toe cleavage,' and all that?"

It was De's turn to look brutally uncomfortable. "Cher

and I are just here to . . . research an environmental project," she stammered, way unconvincingly.

Murray totally guffawed. "Yeah, right. For one thing, Enviropalooza's over, woman. And for another, look at you. You're dressed to kill, baby, and it ain't the beach bacteria on your hit list."

Then he stopped laughing.

It happened all at once. Murray's eyes suddenly fell on De's necklace. Hers fell on the bulging side pocket of his Istante chinos. As De went to grab what was obviously a paperback book from his pocket, she fell head over Manolo Blahniks in the sand. Murray dropped his flowers and his blanket as he bounded over to help her up. *Sense and Sensibility* tumbled out of his pocket.

Okay, so rocket science probably wasn't in De's future. Or mine, either, based on how long it took to dawn upon us both that Jordan wasn't Jordan at all. He was . . .

"Murray??!!"

"Dionne??!!"

"You're . . . Jordan??"

"You're . . . nah! You're . . . *Jasmine?*"

The expressions on their faces morphed from shock, to anger, to the purest form of love as I have ever seen, on screen or in real life.

"Baby . . . I didn't know . . ."

"I never knew . . ."

"Why didn't you say something . . . ?"

"You never told me . . ."

"That's how you felt . . ."

The face-sucking was prodigious. They only surfaced intermittently for air.

I sighed as I turned back toward the street. De and Murray had been Velcroed together forever. How was it possible they knew so little about each other? Not to minimize my influence, but a vacation in cyberspace patched them.

Okay, so normally at moments like these, I would have called a cab. And I was about to, but call me mental, this feeling of needing to be around someone I actually knew washed over me. Someone who, even if I couldn't stand him, did have a driver's license. I whipped out my cell and called Josh.

Chapter 13

*O*pening Night at the Fashion Café was perilously close. And we still had, like, nothing to wear. De, Amber, and I had done Segal, Hayman, Chanel, and Giorgio, plus a multitude of malls, in our manifest destiny quest to pull together the most chronic ensembles.

"If we only knew the shade of crimson of that carpet," Amber whined.

"If we only knew what Elle was wearing," De chimed.

I reminded them, "Girlfriends, you're losing sight of the big picture. At the end of the day will we not be the freshest faces in the place? Will we not be the youngest Bettys? News bulletin: In the world of international press, it's the hot new thing everyone clamors for, and at opening night of the Fashion Café, that means us."

Amber was all, "I see a wall of cameras—focused on us!"

"And not to forget," I said, "we'll be posing next to our own exhibit. Like how do you spell photo op? 'High School Bettys Teach World About Fashion and the Environment.' It's way *People* magazine's 'Star Tracks' column."

"And *Vanity Fair*'s 'Vanities' . . . and . . ."

De panicked. "I feel a three-alarm zit coming on."

Like Alanis says in her famous song "Isn't it ironic," a clarifying call from style-challenged Mackenzie helped us nail the proper ensembles.

"Why not just wear what you wore in the fashion show? You do remember the environmental aspect of this, Cher, don't you?" Mack wasn't being sarcastic. And she had—hello!—turned on a major light bulb.

"The credit card-diskette dress!" De screamed joyously.

"The CD dress!" I shouted, high-fiving her.

Then we both looked at Amber. Like what did that leave for her? I could not hold myself back. "And you, Amber—where's that banyan tree costume now that you really need it?"

De and I totally dissolved in a giggle fit.

Amber, what a surprise, failed to see the humor. She was all, "Excuse me, I have a plethora of ensembles I could wear. I only went shopping with you to lend my expertise."

De and I just made the *W* sign. "Whatever!"

Everything was melding. Geist and Hall were back on lovey-dovey turf. Together, they had totally overseen final execution and delivery of our exhibit to the Fashion Café. They even planned on attending the opening night viewing. I recommended an elegant yet indigenous

Perry Ellis for him and a moderately priced but teacheresque Ellen Tracy for her.

And in appreciation for all the new business, the company I'd hired for my limo pools graciously offered all of Cher's Crewsaders and Amber's Angels free rides to the Fashion Café. Best of all, I'd convinced Mack to come to opening night with us. And to wear a dress. Major accomplishment.

Whenever I thought of Mack, naturally, I thought of Josh. They were like the only blight on my stellar matchmaking record. No matter how often I threw them together, sparks did not ignite. No matter what glowing accolades I heaped on one about the other, all I got back were puzzled looks and perfunctory "That's nice." "Really? Cool." How could they not see how right they were for each other?

Giving up is majorly not me. So I suggested that on opening night, Mack might want to come over to my house and we'd get ready together. I didn't tell her the part about Josh being able to see this total transformation happening before his very eyes. He had to fall for her then.

Only? He didn't. But he should have. For Mack did bike over, and not to be immodest? I did help transform her from ethereal girl to fashional girl. The totally organic makeup was my idea, but the dress Mack had, a sleeveless Jil Sander turtleneck, she brought over herself. It was massively stellar.

"Where'd you get this?" I asked, playfully adding, "This is so not Second Hand Rose."

Mack blushed. "Actually, Susan picked it out for me."

"Susan? As in the evil stepmother?"

"One and the same."

"She's got a good eye for what's right for you," I acknowledged admiringly.

Mack grimaced, so I added, "I mean, I know she could never take the place of your mother, but you have to admit, she kinda does seem to be trying."

Just then the doorbell rang, and I heard Josh yell, "Cher, your ride is here."

"Tell them we'll be right there!" I yelled back.

That Josh was in the foyer was serendipitous. I practically pushed Mack down the steps so he'd still be there. And he was, only I don't think he had his contacts in. Or something.

Instead of being totally blown away by the revamped Mackenzie, he was all, "Don't the two of you look, uh, cute?"

"Is that the best you can do?" I demanded. "Surely your university education has provided you with alternate adjectives."

"Cher—hurry up! We're all waiting for you!" It was Amber, shouting from the limo in the driveway. She, De, Murray, and Sean had already been picked up. I gave Josh a few more seconds to appreciate us, then shrugged my Amex-ed shoulders and led Mack to the stretch.

The scene at the opening was everything I dreamed it would be. I was massively pumped as our limo edged toward the entrance. A phalanx of huge cameras rimmed the periphery. A sea of autograph-seeking generics was held back behind ropes. Because there was a lineup of limos before us, it would be a while before we'd get there. Not wanting to miss anything, Murray and Sean stood up on the seat, slid open the skylight, and hoisted themselves through.

"That's so tacky! Get down!" Amber implored.

She got no support from De, all cushy in her seat, going, "Ain't Murray cute?"

The boys got an eyeful of who was being dispatched from the limos ahead of us. Sporadically they ducked back in the car with reports.

"I saw Elle! Oh, man, I'm in love!" Sean shouted. "Elle baby—I'm here for ya!"

"There's Claudia! Oh, no, she's with that magician dude!" Murray actually sounded disappointed. Like he thought he had a chance?

We crept up to the entrance amid shouts of "Naomi! Look over here!" and "Christy, this way!" But when Murray yelled, "Hey, it's Tom Cruise!" Amber jumped up and stuck her head out the skylight, yelling, "Tommy! Rescue me!"

"Amber, I cannot believe you did that!" I squealed when she settled back into her seat.

"He's short." Amber turned up her nose and sniffed. "Wake me when Brad gets here."

I was about to tell her that he was short, too, when Murray announced, "Our turn, ladies," as the stretch finally pulled up to the front door.

It was way Sharon Stone at the Oscars. As soon as we were dispatched, we were crushed in a sea of journalists. I tossed my hair back and got ready for my moment, just as a ponytailed dude shoved an *ET* microphone into my face, breathlessly asking, "Are you anybody?"

"Hello? I'm Cher!" I replied.

I could not believe what happened next. He totally snorted derisively and sneered, "Cher! You're not Cher. You don't even look like her! That's a good one!" With a smirk, he turned to De. "And I bet you think in that CD dress you're Dionne Warwick."

Amber, who'd never learned to take a hint, instead took that as her cue. She totally got in his face with a self-important "I'm Amber . . ."

Her misguided efforts were met with a jeering, "Right. Valletta's about five inches taller than you, honey, and a whole lot more grown up, if ya catch my drift." Our Amber, like, imploded.

Then, in a vicious display of massive rudeness, he turned to all the camera people and announced dismissively, "Forget it, they're no one."

De's jaw dropped. "No one! I'm calling my mother! She's a publicist!"

Amber sputtered, "Well, excuse me, you're not exactly Bob Goen! Or even John Tesh! Or Mary Hart, either!"

But I don't think he heard her—he was already running after like, some Jurassic star, yelling, "Ivana! Over here!"

"I have never, in all my life, been shunted aside so rudely!" Amber fumed.

"Guess we're not famous enough for the microphone-wielding, butt-kissing, friends-of-Jay-Leno paparazzi," Murray groused.

"Forget it," I said. "Let's go inside. Once we find our exhibit and pose by it, just wait—they'll all come running. They'll be tripping all over themselves trying to get our picture."

"Yeah, then we'll decide who's anybody!" De was still steaming as she whipped out her cellular to call her mother.

Inside, the Fashion Café was rampantly high glam. It was riddled with vertically enhanced models, surgically enhanced celebrities, and their ego-enhanced entourages. The exhibits were impressive. They hung on the walls in all these eclectic alcoves and breakfast nooks that represented such fashion capitols as Milan, Paris, New York, and Beverly Hills. But my favorite area was the room with the carved-in-stone ceiling. It was way Mt. Rushmore with the 3-D visages of Claudia, Naomi, Elle, and Christy peering down at us. I wondered if they had to rechisel it every time someone had plastic surgery.

"Ohmygosh, there's the dress Audrey Hepburn wore in *Breakfast At Tiffany's*." De dragged me over to see it. Amber was more impressed with Madonna's bustier from the Blonde Ambition Tour. Then she drew our attention to the raised catwalk that ran down the center of the restaurant.

"Girlfriends! Look what's comin' down the catwalk." A studly waiter balancing a tray of edibles winked as he got to us. "Care for an hors d'oeuvre?" he offered.

"Don't drool on the food, Amber," I warned.

Murray was still all huffing and puffing, "Oh, I guess even nobodies get to eat."

We would have, too, but we got distracted by the huge video screen featuring an array of Baldwins, with the tag line "Meet the Men of Boss Models."

I searched for Tai, Summer, Jackson, and Jesse, but it was hard to spot anyone under those bean-pole models and stars. I couldn't tell exactly who was there, but I totally heard the names Sharon, Julia, Kevin, and Matthew being bandied about. At least one Friend had arrived, because the generic background music had suddenly switched to "I'll Be There for You."

We were totally trippin', going from alcove to nook,

when Mack suddenly whirled around to me and said, "Where's our exhibit?"

Oops, in all the excitement, we'd almost forgotten. "Maybe in the next room?" I guessed.

Mack placed her arms on her hips and said evenly, "We've trolled every part of this place, Cher, and I know I haven't seen it."

"Let's go ask," I suggested.

"Ask who? You think Claudia would know?" Amber said, advancing toward the back of Claudia's head.

"As if Miss Supermodel Thing would give us the time of day?" De snapped. "We're nobody, remember?"

"Get over it, girlfriend," I said to De. "Don't let them ruin your moment."

"That woman over there"—Mack, the tallest of us, pointed out a frizzy-haired lady—"she's holding a clipboard. Maybe it's a master guide to the exhibits."

Mack had nailed it. But Clipboard Lady looked up and down her list like, five times, going, "The Bronson Alcott exhibit? Is he a new designer? I don't seem to . . ."

Amber was ready to rip the list out of her hands when Clipboard Lady finally said, "Oh, that high school thing—here it is, I found it. Sorry. It's down one level." She pointed at a circular staircase in the rear of the Milan Room.

"That totally explains it. There's another level!" I said triumphantly.

"Our exhibit is probably in the VIP section!" Amber exclaimed.

"Roped off," Sean said excitedly.

"With bouncers guarding it," Murray added. Even he was getting pumped again.

We started down the stairs eagerly. I could not wait to

see what other exhibits ours was placed with. Placement is, like, so rampantly important.

But it was strangely silent as we descended farther down the swirling stairway. I didn't see one sign leading to the VIP section. No roped-off area, no bouncers. No supermodels, celebs, or VIPs in sight.

"Maybe we're on the wrong level?" Sean guessed.

But then we saw Miss Geist. And Mr. Hall. And Tai, Jackson, Summer, and Jesse. Pumped is not exactly how I would describe them. At first I thought they were staring at the door to the ladies' room, and I wondered if maybe Naomi had just gone in there.

Not even. What held their rapt and way puzzled attention was our "Recycled Fashion in the Rain Forest" exhibit. It had gotten placement all right—placement to spare. On the upside, it totally commanded the spotlight. In fact it had the spotlight all to itself. On the downside, it was all alone, tacked up on that space between the ladies' room and the door that said Private, Employees Only.

Miss Geist put her arm around me and tried for a soothing, "Well, maybe it's the first one in what will be a whole new level of exhibits. I'm sure they're planning on bringing others to this level after the opening."

Mr. Hall added, "It's not lopsided."

"And everyone who has to use the bathroom will see it," Tai said, trying for hopeful.

"Yeah, everyone in the small-bladder society," Jesse grumbled.

"It's— it's like during lunch in the Quad and it has no one else to sit with it," De said tragically.

Amber, who could relate to that last analogy, went postal first. She stomped her foot and screeched. "I cannot believe the heinous indignity! This is . . . this is . . . segregation!"

Then Murray exploded, "That does it! They call us nobodies! And then they stick us in the toilet! I am not standing still for this! I demand satisfaction!"

Which, in the end, we didn't exactly get. We did get arrested, though.

Chapter 14

Murray's stomping up the stairs, demanding satisfaction, was what started it. Sean ran after him, yelling, "What he said!" The rest of us bolted up after both of them. Everyone, even Miss Geist and Mr. Hall, had worked up to majorly buggin'. But it was Mack who actually brought the authorities into the picture. She was the one, after all, most experienced in demonstrations. And with our help, she totally started one at the Fashion Café's opening night.

Mack's height made her a commanding presence as she railed and rallied, "I demand to see the owner!"

But instead of the supermodels who should have responded, a couple of sweaty sleazoid types, straight out of central casting—with open shirts and gold medallions—came panting over.

"What seems to be the problem with you kids?" the taller one said.

Mack, who was totally striking in the Jil Sander,

shouted, "*This* is the problem! *You* are the problem! This is a sham!"

Murray was about to jump in, but there was no halting the Mack-attack. She was in high gear. "You people don't care about Earth Day or the environment. This whole Environmental Challenge was just a phony ploy to draw attention to your superfluous little theme restaurant!"

"Pipe down, little missy." The shorter sleazoid put his hand up, cautioning, "Lower your voice."

But Mack was into double-digit decibels. "I will not! I want everyone to hear how you conned the public into believing you cared about the environment, when all you care about is . . . is . . . *this!* You lied—to us! And we are the future of this country. You lied to the public *and* you lied to the planet."

Although I, too, was righteously appalled, I wasn't quite as shocked as Mack. I mean, this is Beverly Hills. Hype is what we do.

But Mack is my friend—and she was right. So I piped up as politely as possible. "You have to admit, she has a point. If you cared about the submissions from the high schools, you would have put our exhibit where it could be seen."

Murray saw his chance to jump into the fray. "You dissed us 'cause we're high school students! This whole gig was just marketing-savvy, hype-polluted, spin control! You invited us, you made us sweat for our place here, and now you trash us in the toilet! You lied to us!"

That's when Mack started the chant. And all of us, even Mr. Hall and Miss Geist, joined in, "Hey, Hey, Fashion Café! How many lies did you tell today?"

* * *

All in all? It was a way major scene. We totally snagged the spotlight from Tom, Sharon, Julia, and the random Friend. And we did, finally, get on *ET*.

But that was only when two uniformed—and way chiseled, I might add—cops bolted down the catwalk toward us, shouting, "All right, that's enough. This is over. You'll have to come with us."

"Come with you? As if!" De searched frantically for her cellular.

Jackson sang out, "We're being arrested, man? Excellent!" Still, he made sure no one manhandled Tai.

Jesse was all, "This is bogus! I could shut down the music in here!"

Murray was all, "Get your hands off my woman, man. I want my lawyer!"

Sean was all, "I want his lawyer!"

De was all, "I want my mother!"

Amber was all, "You can't do this!"

Being dragged away in a credit card-diskette dress was a way new experience. As was the back of the paddy wagon. Comfort wasn't its forte.

I leaned forward to the cop in the front seat, who was separated from us by that grated window you see in the movies, and politely said, "You know, upholstering the benches would make for a much more comfortable ride. I could bring swatches." The cop was profoundly unresponsive.

As we brutally bounced along, Mack leaned over to me. "I have something to tell you, Cher."

"I'm basically captive, Mack," I reminded her. "We all are."

"Remember what you said about my stepmother

choosing the dress and all . . . and how I didn't seem, you know, grateful?"

Mack's dress wasn't exactly what I was thinking about right then, but now that she mentioned it, her expression had been pained when I'd noted the props Susan had done for her.

"It didn't make me think any less of you, Mack, if that's what's buggin' you. Steprelations, as a whole, are one giant pain. I totally speak from experience on the topic."

"No, that's not it, Cher. It's a little more complicated. Susan's okay, she makes my dad happy. And she tries to be nice to us. Only she doesn't exactly support my commitment to the environment."

"She seemed way supportive at the Environmental Expo," I reminded Mack.

"She liked the fashion show part. That's very her. My real mom wasn't into that stuff. We were very close." Then Mack lowered her eyes and said softly, "She died of lung cancer—and she never had a cigarette in her life. Of course, nobody's willing to admit that the toxins in the environment contributed, but I know that's what happened. That's why, sometimes, I might seem a little over-the-top about this stuff. It's a tribute to my mom. It keeps her memory alive for me." By that point Mack had totally welled up. So had everyone in the back of the paddy wagon.

We all leaned over and gave Mack a major group hug.

We never got to see the inside of the jail. At the precinct the sergeant in charge—who was so totally no Jimmy Smits—pointed at Geist and Hall and bellowed, "You two, over here and fill out these forms. You kids, go call your parents. The pay phone's over there."

Leave it to Sean to sneer, "We don't need no stinking pay phones, we're packin'—" The sergeant leaped up, scaring the daylights out of Sean, who meekly finished, "Cellulars, man, I meant, we're packin' cells."

"Well, I'm not," Mackenzie said softly, and started over to the pay phone.

I stopped her. "Actually, Mack? Wait. You kind of are."

"It's okay, Cher, I don't need to borrow yours."

"No, that's not what I mean. I hadn't planned on giving this to you in exactly these, uh, circumstances, but, whatever." I opened my sequined mini Prada and dug out a gift I'd ordered for Mack from one of those green catalogs.

She was shocked. "You bought me a cellular? Cher, that's very nice, but you know how I feel about that."

"I'm aware, but I think you might like this one. It's connected to Earth Tones, an environmental long-distance phone service. They donate all their profits to environmental campaigns. Even their bills come on recycled paper—with detailed Green Alert updates."

"I—I didn't know they had these kinds of cellulars," Mack stammered.

"Well, now you do. Go ahead, call your dad. And Susan."

As expected, all our 'rents were majorly supportive, even Mack's stepmom. It was almost as if she was looking for a way to show Mack that she loved her.

Naturally, Daddy was way proud of me. "You protested shabby treatment? And you learned a chant? That's my girl!"

Even though the Fashion Café did not press charges, they totally did not offer restitution, either. Our exhibit stayed put. But our protest was like, "Our top story tonight" on the entertainment news shows. Even *House of Style* covered it. It was massively cool the way Shalom Harlow and Amber Valletta showed clips, commenting favorably on our ensembles. Although, tragically, it turned out our Amber was right after all—Shalom's mole is brutally faux.

All the talk shows invited us to come on, but as a group we overruled Amber and opted for a tasteful press release, prepared by De's mom. I'm majorly proud to say that we used our fifteen minutes of fame in a positive, solution-oriented manner. Instead of bemoaning our shabby treatment, we wrote about how the earth massively needs all of us, and what we can do to bring attention to the way important cause of a clean, green planet.

There was another bodacious bonus to our entire brouhaha. It helped reunite Mack with her trail-mix posse.

"It was pretty weird the way it all happened," Mack admitted to me and De a few weeks later. We were in the Quad, tossing our peach pits into the compost heap. "But my friends are finally convinced that there is more than one way to get things done. They won't come out and say it, but I think they realize that my alliance with you brought a lot of positive attention to our cause. Not to mention, look how much got done. And—oh, I can't believe I forgot to tell you!—I got a letter from the city council yesterday. It looks like our tree ordinance might actually pass!"

"Mackenzie! That's so righteous!" I jumped up and hugged her.

"I'm totally kvelling!" De added. We did a three-way high five.

Then I said slyly, "Did I not tell you Josh could help?"

Josh and Mack. All my plans for bringing them together had totally tanked. As in, glug, glug, glug. As in *The Cable Guy*. But if I had to concede defeat, I was determined to find out why. I'd totally gotten nowhere with the stepdrone. My only choice was to ask Mack directly.

"Uh, speaking of Josh . . . did you even like him at all?"

Mack grinned her lopsided grin. "Josh is fine, Cher. He's smart, compassionate, and dedicated to the environment. He's a good egg."

"As in . . . poached?" De asked.

Mack laughed. "No, as in good people. Josh is good people—and a good influence on you, I might add."

"But don't you think he's also a hottie?" I glanced at De.

Mack sighed. "Look, I'm not completely oblivious, and neither is Josh. But despite your best efforts at matchmaking—"

I was profoundly shocked. "It was that obvious?"

"Like the hole in the ozone layer!" Mack grinned.

"So, you two didn't hook up because of me?" I asked.

"It had nothing to do with you, Cher—one way or the other. Josh and I just didn't click. It takes more than sharing the same values, don't you know that?" Mack chuckled. "I once asked my mom why she married Dad—they were so different. And Mom just laughed and said it's all about chemistry. And that love is beautiful, mysterious, and often where you least expect it. In fact, sometimes it's opposites that attract and make the best couples."

I was about to protest, like, that's not always true, when Mack added, "Look, you and I are complete opposites in lots of ways, right? Yet I think we formed a friendship here, don't you?"

A few weeks later I was sprawled out on my rain-forest-inspired—as if!—canopy bed, reading *Vanity Fair*, when my complete and utter opposite came swinging in to my room.

"Too bad about the Fashion Café," he said without a trace of sarcasm, "but I guess there is a strange kind of justice after all."

"Don't tell me you actually care about the heinously unfair placement of our stellar exhibit?" I said, without looking up.

"Your placement? No, I mean, too bad that the entire theme restaurant is being torn down."

I finally peered up at Josh. "What are you talking about?"

"Don't you read the papers, Cher?"

"Not usually."

"Well, then, here, catch up." Josh tossed himself and the *LA Times* onto my bed. The headline read, "Fashion Café to Be Torn Down: Archaeologists Find Ancient Native American Burial Site Below It."

I read aloud, " 'Environmentalists, once considered a fringe group in Beverly Hills, are newly powerful in our area due to the successful effort to curb cruise-ship dumping. A coalition of environmentalists recently exerted pressure to tear down the just-opened theme restaurant when it was discovered to have been constructed on an ancient Native American burial site.'

" 'While representatives from the Fashion Café declined comment, leading student environmentalist Amber Salk had this to say, "Excuse me, it serves them right. They totally lied to us, we, the very future of our country. And hello? They made a sham of opening night. Not to mention, the hors d'oeuvres were lacking." ' "

My jaw dropped. "They quoted Amber! As a leading environmentalist." I sputtered, "As if!"

Josh grinned, rolled up the newspaper, and tapped me on the head with it. "Lighten up, Cher, and look at the big picture. The Fashion Café dissed you, and now they're out of business. As you would say, it's like that famous quote 'All's well that ends well.' "

I looked at Josh for signs of cynicism. There were none.

About the Author

Randi Reisfeld is the author of *Clueless™: An American Betty in Paris* and *Clueless™: Cher's Furiously Fit Workout*. She is currently working on *Who's Your Fave Rave? 40 Years of 16 Magazine*, as well as several other works of young adult fiction and celebrity biographies.

She lives in the New York area with her family.